HAPPINESS IS A CHEMICAL IN THE BRAIN

"The stories read somewhat like a distaff version of Raymond Carver . . . but Ms. Perillo is expressive where Carver is laconic, and her characterizations, particularly of men, can be as darting and lethal as snakebites." —Sam Sacks, *Wall Street Journal*

"Emotionally unflinching stories of considerable power, wonder and humor." —*Kirkus Reviews*, starred review

"Raw, relentless and eye-opening." —*Publishers Weekly*, Best Books of 2012

"These tales are as beautifully patterned as poetry, as saturated in feeling, open to ambiguity, and laced with electrifying images." —Donna Seaman, *Booklist*, starred review

"[Perillo] strikes a glorious balance between wryly intelligent prose and emotional force, recalling Alice Munro at her best." —*Publishers Weekly*, starred review

"Bleak, foreboding, oddly intimate." —*Ms.*

"Very funny and often beautiful . . . reminds us that there's a lasting (if messy) beauty in the way we collide with each other, however briefly." —Katie Haegele, *Philadelphia Inquirer*

"A collection of wonders that readers will devour with immediacy . . . stunning in its precision and imagery." —Alison Espach, *Fiction Writers Review*

"Relentlessly compassionate, this is a collection for the mistake makers and trying-as-hard-as-we-canners of the world—which probably means all of us." —Leigh Newman, Oprah.com

ALSO BY LUCIA PERILLO

POETRY

Dangerous Life

The Body Mutinies

The Oldest Map with the Name America

Luck Is Luck

Inseminating the Elephant

On the Spectrum of Possible Deaths

NONFICTION

I've Heard the Vultures Singing:
Field Notes on Poetry, Illness, and Nature

HAPPINESS
IS A
CHEMICAL
IN THE
BRAIN

STORIES

LUCIA PERILLO

 W. W. NORTON & COMPANY · NEW YORK · LONDON

Copyright © 2012 by Lucia Perillo

For information about permission to reproduce selections from this book,
write to Permissions, W. W. Norton & Company, Inc.,
500 Fifth Avenue, New York, NY 10110

For information about special discounts for bulk purchases, please contact
W. W. Norton Special Sales at specialsales@wwnorton.com or 800-233-4830

Manufacturing by Courier Westford
Book design by Iris Weinstein
Production manager: Julia Druskin

Library of Congress Cataloging-in-Publication Data

Perillo, Lucia Maria, 1958–
Happiness is a chemical in the brain : stories / Lucia Perillo. — 1st ed.
        p. cm.
ISBN 978-0-393-08353-8 (hardcover)
1. Northwest, Pacific—Fiction. 2. City and town life—Fiction. I. Title.
PS3566.E69146H37 2012
813'.54—dc23

                                    2012001613

ISBN 978-0-393-34546-9 pbk.

W. W. Norton & Company, Inc.
500 Fifth Avenue, New York, N.Y. 10110
www.wwnorton.com

W. W. Norton & Company Ltd.
Castle House, 75/76 Wells Street, London W1T 3QT

1 2 3 4 5 6 7 8 9 0

CONTENTS

HAPPINESS
IS A
CHEMICAL
IN THE
BRAIN

BAD BOY NUMBER SEVENTEEN

Don't tell me about bad boys. I've seen my black clouds come and go. Coming they walk with their shoulders back like they've got a raw egg tucked inside each armpit, and they let their legs lead them. Going, you can count on the fact that their butts will cast no shadow on those lean long legs. You can't compete in the arena of squalid romance if you're one of those guys shaped in the rear like a leather mail sack: you're automatically disqualified. That's just the way it is. I didn't make the rules.

My prodigals make up for slender means by wearing their jeans tight enough so that their billfolds have a hard time sliding in. And they make up for the fact they're usually kind of stupid by not saying much. This is important. This is the litmus test. The last thing you want is a desperado with a big mouth; you might as well invite a wild elephant home for dinner.

See, for years I have done some serious observation, up close and from a distance. I've seen them hawk and spit before the drive-up window, I've watched them jimmy the pinball machine at King Arthur's Reef. Yeah, yeah: I know King Arthur had a table, he didn't have a reef, but ours is a coastal town and the natives feel claustrophobic inside any bar that doesn't have a nautical theme. Why it matters I don't know, because inside is always dim—so you can't see that the only decorating theme is duct tape, which holds the stuffed fish to the walls and crisscrosses the red vinyl in the booths, and even bandages some of the more expensive bottles of liquor that no one has the heart to throw away because of something as picayunish as a little broken glass.

But out of all the dives in town, the Reef is probably the best laboratory for studying the players, the wannabes with their ball caps and Aerosmith T-shirts, and the shy bloodhounds who rest their elbows on the bar and silently massage their dewlaps. Inside every dissolute romantic there's a brooding Schopenhauer, with a chronic melancholy that he nurses like a sourball in his cheek. He can see the whole arc of his life—from the uphill curve that is his present freedom to the downhill slope that'll lead him to some evangelical storefront church where he'll suddenly find himself swaying with his hands raised in the air. And the ones who come without this flaring sense of precognition are just losers, plain and simple.

Like one night in the Reef there's this guy sitting on a barstool, checking me out over his shoulder from time to time? The fact that he's missing part of one finger shrouds him with the kind of mystery that ought to make him a contender, were this aura not counteracted by his jeans riding so low they expose a length of his crack that's about equal to what's missing from his hand. Which knocks him out of the running, especially when a few boilermakers later he erupts in my direction with something about letting him know whenever I'm ready to have him take me outside to his car, where he's going to—his phrasing—*eat me out*.

I'm sitting in a booth with my sister Louisa, who giggles. "Don't giggle," I tell her. "What that guy said to us wasn't funny." Even though she's my older sister, since she has Down syndrome I have to explain everything.

"I think he's funny," she says in that woofy voice of hers. "I think he's cute. I think that boy wants to be my boyfriend."

This is the kind of thing Louisa'll say that drives a stake into our mother's heart. Lately Mum's been talking about getting Louisa's tubes tied, a plan I could condone on pragmatic grounds but against which I've nonetheless felt compelled to launch a squeak or two of protest. Louisa's been living with Mum ever since she got kicked out of the group home for repeated makeup theft, and even though Louisa's relatively self-sufficient—she can ride the bus, she has a job assembling calendars and pens—my mother won't rest easy until Louisa's fate is sewn up. I mean, Louisa needs a baby about as badly as she needs a scholarship to MIT, but then part of me says: What right do we have to go monkeying around with Louisa's body? Since when did we set up camp between her legs? I even feel squeamish bringing Louisa into the bar, like someone's going to call Child Protective Services on me, though Louisa's well past thirty. When the bartender checks our IDs she lingers for a long time with

Louisa's, her eyes ping-ponging between the mug shot and Louisa's face.

After a few moments of scrutiny the bartender slides her ID across the table. "What does she want?" the bartender asks me.

One thing Louisa's figured out is this what-to-do-when-people-refuse-to-speak-to-you routine. "Beer!" she pipes angrily.

"You want me to bring her a light beer?"

"St. Pauli Girl," Louisa insists. Where she gets this from I don't know. *St. Pauli Girl.* But the bartender's still looking at me.

"Hey, I'm her sister, not her mother. Give her what she wants. She's not the one driving." And I order a St. Pauli Girl for myself too, just so Louisa won't get paranoid that she's done something weird.

Anyway, the bartender vindicates herself later, by taking care of Finger when he makes his suggestion about taking me outside. Or maybe this is ego talking, my assuming that Finger was bird-dogging me and not my sister, who is after all not a bad-looking woman, especially with her new perm and John Lennon eyeglass frames. I guess the bartender decides to step in as Louisa's protectress since she thinks I'm being too lax about that job. Bartender says something to Finger underneath her breath, something threatening enough to make his eyes go wide. Then to soothe us all she takes a bunch of change from the till and drops it into the jukebox.

This does the trick: the bar falls silent while the lead guitar knifes its way through the intro. Then, with the grace and synchronicity of ballerinas, all the guys start playing air guitar by strumming the folds of skin around their navels. Finger tilts woozily over his glass, and by the time the song ends his arms are folded on the bar with his head nested inside, whistling the strange birdcalls of sleep.

"Look," Louisa says, elbowing me. "That funny boy is sleeping."

"I told you he's not funny. He's a jerk."

"Yeah," she says, bobbing her head. Often I find myself wishing Louisa did not agree so enthusiastically with everything I say. It forces me to police myself all the time, and this policeman speaks in a voice I recognize as belonging to my mother, who'll say (as in defense of turning off Louisa's plumbing), *I wish you would start considering your sister's future more seriously. All I'm trying to do is set things up so that Louisa will be less of a burden when the day comes that neither I nor your father are around.*

My mother always gives the words *your father* an extra jab. He has a new wife who lives with him in a house overlooking the Tacoma Narrows and the bridge that replaced the one they call Galloping Gertie because it turned into Jell-O on a particularly windy day. My mother, on the other hand, is stuck living with Louisa in a trailer, though she becomes offended when I refer to it as such. "It's a *mobile home,*" she insists huffily. "And I've got the clubhouse. I notice you don't mind coming down off your high horse whenever you want to use the pool."

As you can tell, it's a sore subject—my mother stuck with

a clubhouse whose lone assets are a machine that dispenses last year's Ho Hos, and a pool that can barely accommodate a decent cannonball, while my father's got Galloping Gertie II and the whole of Puget Sound right in his living room. My mother thought she could salve her pride by hiring a decorator, whose handiwork ended up making the trailer look like the set of a late-night TV talk show, which must remind Louisa all the more about how her life has paled ever since she had to leave the group home, where she could tussle with her girlfriends on the battered furniture every night, like attending summer camp forever. Louisa is simply too big for my mother's place—and it's not so much her fatness as the way that her high spirits make her seem loud and clumsy. And my mother takes them as evidence of Louisa's naïveté and thinks we must band together to fend off evil.

"Look, Louisa," I say, watching Finger's drool run from his downhill cheek. "You've got to start looking out for yourself. There's a lot of boys out there who are not nice boys."

Her face darkens. "Like the boys who yell at me at the bus stop. Mummy says they aren't nice."

"You know what I call them? Creeps." And then I ask her, "What did Mum tell you to do about them?"

Louisa answers ambivalently, and I can tell that despite their terrors the bus stop boys still glitter. "Mummy said just ignore them. She said for me to pretend their voices are the wind." This she demonstrates by blowing our cocktail napkins off the table.

"Goodbye, creeps!" Louisa whooshes.

∽

NOW, LET ME CONFESS I haven't always proved to be the shrewdest judge of human nature. My romances have left me with a recurring dream in which I'm slashing tires and the tires' blood is spilling out. In my freshman year of high school I encountered Bad Boy Number One, who had me doing his pre-algebra problems half the night while he worked out the science of breaking-and-entering. Number Two was old enough to drive a car, and this romance (with the car more than the boy per se) left me with a greenstick fracture of my collarbone. Number Six was the one who suckered me into cosigning the loan on his new Mustang—how this story ends you don't need me to say—and Number Eight was the proud owner of a set-yourself-up-in-the-creative-and-lucrative-world-of-tattooing-with-EZ-monthly-payments kit, which he'd ordered from the back of a comic book.

Don't ask me why I couldn't see he had loser written all over him, not until after I let him go to work on my left arm, on a rattlesnake whose rattle he inked on the inside of my elbow. It was supposed to be a little snake, but Number Eight had not yet mastered his craft, and the tail came out blotched and broken. Which compelled Number Eight to keep on keeping on, zigzagging it down the length of my forearm so that he could get the most practice in. No way I could shut him down without leaving a lopped-off reptile on my body, and by the time he got to my wrist I have to admit the snake was starting to look pretty good, and the head—which he ran onto the back of my hand, too large for the rest of its body by half—was a masterpiece, with a mosaic of scales and a flicking tongue.

Number Eight OD'd on a speedball when the snake was just about complete but for the eye sockets that he hadn't gotten around to filling, which was about the same time I realized that putting a snake's head on your hand means that you have chosen an idiosyncratic road to head down in life, unless you plan to wear little white gloves all the time like Mr. Peanut. Though a butterfly or a rose won't raise anyone's brow, Bad Snake gives you a hundred demerits in all but a few select kinds of job interviews; where they finally took me in was at the boat shop. Boat people have a tendency to forgive what other people might consider sluttishness. There are few sluts in the boat world, the way there are few sluts at the Handy Rental, or working in Accounts Payable at Karl's Kustom Kar Kustomizing, maybe because these industries top-heavy with losers are willing to extend women a quid pro quo of retroactive grace.

Of course, the tattoo was what convinced my mother I had finally gone around the bend: ever since, she's been afraid I have an unsettling influence on Louisa. Her preference would be for the two of us not to be left alone, but she waffles on this because I am Louisa's cheapest chaperone. When mum wanted to go on a cruise, for instance, she had no choice but to ask me to move into the trailer for two weeks. This makes Louisa happy because she knows we'll turn the radio up full blast and eat from Styrofoam clamshells of take-out food and launch into a cleaning frenzy just minutes before my mother walks back through the door.

So I'm staying there on a drizzly Sunday, when what Louisa wants to do is see a movie. We commit the ultimate sin by spreading the newspaper out on the white carpet, and after Louisa scrutinizes the movie ads her finger stabs one called *Primal Reflex*, starring Hollywood's latest flavor-of-the-month in some pretty steamy scenes. At junctures like these my mother's voice cuts in, and I point out the comedies instead.

Louisa's mind is made up. "I want to see this girl do the hula-hula," she says. In the advertisement, Latest Flavor's got a hibiscus flower pinned behind one ear, her face framed in the crosshairs of a gun.

"It's not a hula movie," I explain. "You're thinking of like Annette Funicello."

"No. I'm thinking of *her*." Louisa trots into her room to retrieve a movie magazine that's got a picture of Flavor wearing a lei and a thong bikini, bodysurfing off the coast of Waikiki.

"Toldja," Louisa says.

∼

WITH LOUISA, you can never go into the obvious, the *this has nothing to do with anything, oh my dearest darling one*. Louisa's brain moves like a jackrabbit, and when she's threatened she uses the jackrabbit's zigzag to escape. Like after she makes her point, Louisa immediately starts preparing, digging out this folding plastic rainhat Mum gave her last Christmas. *What kind of gift*, I said, *do you call a piece of plastic that you got free from the beauty shop?*—to which my mother sniped that Louisa wouldn't know the difference. And it irked me to realize my mother had been right, because the rainhat is one of Louisa's prized possessions. She wears it proudly as we board the bus downtown, which I suggest in order to make the trip seem like more of an adventure. Or maybe I'm subconsciously stalling so we'll have to catch the three-fifteen show instead, which features dogs that speak with famous voices.

No luck: we get there right on time, and during the movie I hear Louisa giggle whenever the woman appears naked on-screen. Of course, we don't get to see the men naked, and for once I'm grateful for Hollywood's injustices. Afterward Louisa gives the movie two thumbs up and can't wait to boogie—*I want a happy beer*, she says, the Reef being just a few blocks from the theater.

When I give her all my quarters for the jukebox, my sister punches in a rock-and-roll number called "Jesus Is Just Alright" and comes back to the table knowing all the words, which surprises me because I've never heard Louisa say anything about Jesus. Our mother sometimes drags her to the Church of the Parted Waters, a Baptist outfit Mum joined because of its zeal for coffee klatches and potlucks, though often she returns home with her own dishes barely touched.

I think the Baptists are afraid my mother's hexed: why else would she have given birth to a Down's kid when she was only in her twenties, the other one don't even mention—they've heard about the snake. I also suspect Mum's main interest in the church is that she thinks it'll dignify the ugly rituals of cruising men. She's sailing to Nassau with the Baptists as we speak, even though I didn't have the heart to tell her what any woman with two working eyeballs should be able to see: that the Church of the Parted Waters is a magnet for losers. And I mean the capital-*L* Losers—we're talking bankruptcy and Thorazine. Personally I think she's got better odds of scoring heroin among them than a husband.

But I should talk. I'm not even going to tell you about Black Clouds Nine through Sixteen, though my not mentioning them doesn't mean they're not etched permanently in my brain along with all the ways I behaved shamelessly in their presence. They're printed inside my skull with such big block letters that when the next one walks into the Reef—and I know he's the next one, don't ask how I know—the word rolls up my throat and into my mouth without the slightest calculation. *Seventeen.* Straightaway that culprit gland starts spewing acid in my gut.

A few days ago, I'd shown him the half dozen used boats we had sitting on the lot. I trailed behind so I could make a careful study of his hips, and now, as he's walking in, I get the full-on view: black T-shirt with a breast pocket, breast pocket with a cigarette pack, cigarette pack a quarter full and crumpled. Right away he recognizes me and sits down to give me an update, something like, *Yesterday I decided on the Bayliner and went over and gave Milty some money down. What I liked about the Bayliner was that it came stocked with this Mercury outboard that you could tear down with both eyes closed and one arm tied behind your back.*

I say, *Let me see if the gasoline smell's still on your hand.* No, just kidding, I don't say that—the last thing he wants is a woman who's off her rocker, despite that urban legend about the secret sexual positions known only to female lunatics.

"You got a good buy," I say. And something like: "We haven't had that Bayliner for a week." The reason I have a hard time tracking what we say is because Louisa's sitting beside me, singing "Jesus Is Just Alright" with her eyes closed. In a place like the Reef a woman singing won't turn anybody's head, at least not until she starts a fistfight, but when Louisa finally opens her eyes and sees Seventeen, her face flushes purple as an eggplant.

"Keep singing," he says. "You sing good."

Louisa's afraid he's teasing. "Naw . . ." she demurs.

But he says, "No really, I like this song. And when it comes on the radio I can never understand the words because the guy mumbles. But you don't mumble. Shoot, you sing better than he does."

This must be one of Louisa's all-time famous moments. She trembles but retains enough composure to keep singing, and after the song's over Seventeen applauds and volunteers to buy us all another round.

Reading the label on Louisa's bottle, he whistles. "You got expensive taste, sister."

It's a word Louisa grabs on to joyfully. "I'm her big sister," she announces, elbowing me. "I get to boss her around."

"I bet you do," he says. The beer comes; he and I pass the time debating the merits of Mercury versus Evinrude outboards while Louisa beams in and out of the conversation. When he goes to the can, Louisa leans toward me and says, "I think this one will be my boyfriend."

"Oh, yeah? How can you tell?"

"I think he's nice to me."

It's Mum talking when I hear myself say, "Why, you don't know the first thing about that guy," which makes Louisa go silent, tracing out letters in her spilled beer.

Finally she says, "You're my sister, but you know what?" And she goes on to answer herself without looking at me: "You don't always know everything."

~

THE THREE OF US leave the Reef buzzed and giddy from what has been a very happy hour, Louisa with the dopey rainhat accordioned on her head and almost swooning when Seventeen volunteers to tie the plastic flaps in a bow beneath her chin. We're walking to Seventeen's pickup so he can give us a ride home, Louisa hanging on his arm, and though it doesn't seem physically possible, her happiness escalates by yet another order of magnitude when she sees what's bounding in the truck bed: some kind of animal resembling a cross between a mountain goat and an old upholstered chair.

"That's Red," says Number Seventeen. "I bet he's glad to see us."

"He's white!" Louisa declares. "How come you call him Red?"

"Well, I'm glad someone's on her toes. But if I tell you the story you've got to promise you won't cry." As he shoves and scruffs the dog, who's chained to an old tire plus its rim, he tells us how he paid four hundred dollars for a pure-bred he was going to use for hunting ducks ". . . and I ended up with this thing. Now, does this look anything like a golden retriever to you?"

No! No! we shout half drunkenly. And again when he starts to drive us home—*No! No!*—Louisa and I riding in the back with a tarp pulled up to our chins. The truck is just an old rice-burner, and when we all wouldn't fit in the cab I watched Louisa wrestle with her loyalties: she wanted to pat the dog, she wanted to stick with her sister, she wanted to ride up front with the boy who's as glamorous to her as any movie star. In the end that made two against one and Louisa got in back with the dog and me.

"Take us to see the boat!" I holler into the open driver's window. But Seventeen hollers back about how he hasn't picked it up yet.

Instead he takes us to see where he's going to keep it berthed, the air misting just enough that we can feel it on our faces as we lie in the truck bed so no one can see. There's clouds swooshing overhead and firs to our starboard until Steamboat Harbor cuts into them ten miles from town, where the Sound picks up current and breaks into chop, and it's there that Seventeen pulls up in the gravel parking lot. When he comes crunching around the truck bed, he's shouldering a six-pack that he's pulled from behind the seat. "It's shit beer, ladies," he says as he climbs in. "But it's all I got."

Louisa's getting wasted, way past the two-beer limit I usually hold her to. But today I say oh, what the hell: she's happy, the boy is lying underneath the tarp between us, and the dog is nosing the folds of her rainhat—until he discovers skin and starts making big slurps up and down her face.

∾

HERE'S THE LAST THING I learned from my romances: bad boys are lousy lays. Going into it you have to understand they're not the kind of guys who'll care whether or not you come. That part of the equation goes right over their head, the whole idea of female orgasm reminding them of high school math class and having to solve for x. What they do best is look out for themselves, which means popping a beer or falling asleep or—and perhaps this is the epitome of their postcoital tristesse—turning on the TV and discovering a replay of the Indy 500, cars going round and round and round.

This is how the world is starting to look when we finish the last of Seventeen's beer, dusk settling on the water, which seems to whirl in a slow eddy that spins the boats and ricochets the stars. After Seventeen takes us out for cheeseburgers and doesn't even squawk when Louisa uses about forty of those little packs of ketchup, ripping them open with her teeth and shooting the contents in jags that scribble her with red, the three of us end up, where else, at the trailer, where Louisa, despite her happiness or maybe sated with it, falls on the sofa and commences snoring like a man. In my mother's bedroom Seventeen says, *Now you gotta let me see the rest of that snake*, and when I roll up my sleeve he starts to improvise his murmurs . . . *Let's see if you got any other secret pitchers* . . . and I show him it all to prove there's no more pictures.

Let me say flat-out that, despite these promising overtures, sex with Seventeen is not a memorable event. The alcohol makes his athleticism sloppy, and when he touches me he's wide on all his marks. Sure you could heap some of the blame on me, but the woman is generally not held accountable once she's tilted off the upright. And that's not laziness but a female way of lending grace: you've got to give these guys control of one thing when everything else about their lives is veering off its course, the one thing they think is most important, the one thing they think'll turn them into men.

What I'm trying to explain is why I'm not crestfallen in the morning when I discover Number Seventeen is gone. Only for a moment does his vanishing come as a surprise, until I remember that sometime during his examination of my marked and unmarked skin he told me that he'd have to be at a roofing job by six. In fact when I first wake up I think I'm lying in a strange motel until I realize that it's just my mother's bedroom with its Johnny Carson drapes.

And just like in a cheap motel there's this loud thump-crash-thumping coming from the other rooms, where I find

Louisa romping around with Seventeen's beast, who's still chained to the tire that he's dragging across my mother's rug. Already they've broken one wing off the wingback chair, and now he puts his paw right through a sofa cushion as though he were stepping into a bucket. Hanging from his teeth the dog's got some kind of translucent seaweed that I finally realize is Louisa's rainhat.

"What's going on here?" I scream, but Louisa's confused that I could be angry on such a joyful morning. "I think that boy left this nice dog for me." And damned if she's not right: on the counter there's a note that reads, *Didn't want to tell you I am married, etc. Wife has allergies and wanted me to put the dog down yesterday, so maybe it was Red's good luck that I ran into you and your sister, who seems like she could use a hound like him.* Spelling is not Seventeen's best subject; actually the note reads, "I am marred, ect." *I am marred?* And I slap myself when I finally get it—should have known he was married. Said his mother was dead and yet that T-shirt reeked of laundry soap.

I crumple the note and yell for Louisa to throw herself between the dog and the knickknack shelf.

"What's the matter?" Louisa says, too late, as a china lighthouse crashes. "I love this dog." She drapes her body along his length and squeezes his ribs, which causes the dog to spread his legs and discharge a yellow stream.

Too late for either of us to go to work, I call us in sick while Louisa lies on the sofa holding a block of frozen peas to her head while Red laps from the toilet. "I have a *hang-over*," Louisa moans, doling out the word like it's a million bucks. Before noon the toilet's dry and Red is hankering for out, so we take him down to the vacant lot. First I have to take a hacksaw to his chain to cut the tire free, and then Louisa uses a plastic jump rope as a leash, on the end of which he strains and wheezes. Louisa bellows, *Hold on, boy!* as we zigzag down the street.

As soon as we get there and she lets go, Red's bolting across the wasteland like a streak, the spiky late summer wildflowers still in bloom but what does the dog care about that kind of beauty as he tramples it underfoot. Louisa follows in hot pursuit, and soon the two of them are leaping through the field while I hang back at the edge of the street.

"What are you waiting for?" she yells. "Mummy'll be home soon."

Now Red stops to look back at me, his dark eyes flashing, one rear paw scratching up some rocks. I think it's me he wants, but when I step forward his hackle-hair rises. And oh, how these bad boys can snarl.

No, not me, as he trots off in the wake of my sister's dust with a whimper that is musical and soft. And damned if I don't know that trick, how they'll sing you a schmoozey song before they break your heart like a china plate.

But it's no use trying to warn her; she would just think I was trying to keep him for my own private thrill. The thrill of being smashed into and crashing, when he knocks her down and they go rolling through the weeds.

BIG-DOT DAY

"I don't know what I was thinking," Arnie's mother said more than once on the drive out, "Vegas was no place for a child." They'd gone to Las Vegas because of the last guy, and now the new guy thought he could line up work on a salmon fishing boat, which was why they were driving to a place on the Washington coast that his mother kept calling *the end of the earth*. At least one good thing about this place, Arnie figured, would be that if his mother took it into her head to move any farther west they'd have to set sail for China. And his mother usually didn't go in for Chinese guys.

The new guy had been an abrupt transaction. This morning, which was now yesterday morning, Arnie was woken by the crinkling sound of his mother putting his clothes into plastic grocery bags. "You can bring one toy," she said, and he chose a flying lizard that transformed into an attack spaceship. But when she put the bags in the hatchback of their old Datsun, she saw he'd also thrown his fishing pole in.

"I said one toy," she'd objected. "We still have to fit Jay's tools and the TV." But he'd argued that a fishing pole was not the same thing as a toy, and the new guy intervened on his behalf, assuring her that the fishing pole might come in handy.

"Lotta fish in that ocean," he said. "Lotta salmon in those creeks." Arnie knew the new guy's name was Jay, but the old guy's name had been Ray and Arnie was afraid of mixing them up. Like the lizard and the attack ship, they were mostly interchangeable: same body—long-armed, short, and barrel-chested—but with different heads. Over the years, the guys stayed the same age while his mother got older. In this way they were the one constant she maintained.

The new guy had a beard and he drove, their Datsun blowing blue smoke out the back. From the back seat, Arnie saw the Sierras swirling away in a haze of blue mist. The new guy called Arnie "Little Man."

"Yo, Little Man back there, fish me up another pack of cigs."

It was morning when they left, and it was the next morning but earlier still when the Datsun sputtered up the coastal range and finally glided down its westward edge, exiting the firs that closed over the road just as the first light silvered the edges of the bay. Giant brown creatures, standing chest-high in the marsh grass, stared at them as they drove by.

"Elk," said the new guy. "Ain't that something." Arnie's mother was sleeping, slumped against where the window handle would have been if it hadn't broken off. There were dozens of elk, chewing thoughtfully, whisking their tails to reveal their white rumps.

"Hey, whose idea was this?" the new guy said, reaching back between the seats to muss up Arnie's hair.

When the road finally ran out underneath them, they checked into a motel, where Arnie's mother stumbled into bed without ever fully waking. The new guy snored like a car ignition trying to catch, holding out the possibility of something about to happen. Which might not ever happen. For a long while Arnie lay on his own bed and tried to sleep, but couldn't. There was too much bed and it made him feel exposed, as if he were camped out on the desert.

Actually, he'd liked living in the desert, how clean it made him feel. Instead of a lawn they had a whole yard full of white rocks. But in Las Vegas he had missed water, real water and not the fake-o reservoirs stocked with stupid placid perch. He missed the idea of himself living by a creek and him being the boy who sits on the bank of it, fishing. It was something he'd done only a few times, back when they'd lived in Denver, and he'd never caught anything but still he'd liked it. The quietness, sure, but also the promise that fishing made about another world existing right under your nose. A world with animals who could extract the secret air inside of water, using combs they carried in the sides of their own necks. This was how the new guy, Jay, had sold Arnie on the trip, even though it meant leaving the white rocks and all his other stuff behind. Jay had promised him that when they got to the end of the earth there would be lots of fishing.

"First thing we'll do," he said, "I'll take you out to John's River and we'll try our luck at steelhead." He told Arnie about how the fish swam up the creeks to breed, flinging their bodies against the rocks as they hopped from one pool to another. "Like missiles blasted from an underwater sub, I swear," Jay said. "One after another. Bam bam bam bam bam."

This was what he'd said around Tonopah, and all the way west Arnie let himself be teased by the idea of the steelhead. When at last they saw the great beasts standing in the salt marsh, Arnie pictured the fish swimming in between their feet. Tickling, which was why the elk every so often twitched.

"How many'd you catch?" Arnie had asked then.

"Catch what?" Jay's eyes were barely slits. They'd been driving more than twenty hours straight.

"You know. The steelhead."

Arnie's scalp prickled, his hair still mussed from Jay's having rubbed it. Now Jay rubbed his own hair, which was black and thick and hung in ringlets on his neck.

"I never caught any," he admitted. "I never even been here. You're seeing it for the first time same as me."

At this point the salt marsh grew blurry, from tears that Arnie tried to keep the new guy from seeing. He should have guessed that nothing swam down there between the elks' legs. The fish were just a gimmick to get him to come along quietly.

"Aww, Little Man, don't wig out on me," the new guy

said, when he twisted around and saw Arnie crouched behind the seat. "Don't worry, everything'll be great, you'll see."

"If you've never been here, how would you know?"

"I know. I got a cousin who lives out this-away."

≈

IN THE MOTEL, as the margin of light grew larger around the drapes, his mother groaned and knitted herself into the new guy's arms and legs. Eventually she hoisted herself under the sheet to reach for a Styrofoam cup that she'd left on the nightstand.

"Ugh," she said, after taking a swallow. "Hello, Washington. I thought your coffee was supposed to be so great."

"You bought that last night in Oregon," the new guy reminded her, as he took the cup and tossed it into the wastebasket. The cup sailed across the room without spilling a drop, though it left a stain on the wall where it ricocheted before it fell.

She sat up then with the sheet bound across her chest and looked at Arnie.

"How you like it here so far?"

"Okay, I guess."

She was doodling her hand in the curls at the nape of the new guy's neck. Then her voice changed, as if an idea had just occurred to her.

"Hey, Arnie, I bet a smart kid like you could find me

a decent cup of coffee in this town." She fished out a five-dollar bill from her purse that was on the floor beside the bed and made him come around to get it.

"You know how I want it?"

"Lots of cream, lots of sugar," Arnie recited—after all these years, of course he knew.

Their motel room was on the second floor, with a little balcony out one side. On the other side was the door that led to the outside stairs and the parking lot. Now that he was seeing it with a wider angle than the car windows allowed, Arnie realized that the end of the earth was just a spit of sand paved over to keep the wind from blasting it away. Earlier this morning, when they'd passed the salt marsh full of elk, the sun had glimmered just above the mountains, a bright smudge in the gray. But now the clouds were thicker, letting loose a kind of rain that hovered, weightless. He remembered that his coat was still locked in the car, and his sweatshirt grew heavy as it sopped up moisture from the air.

The road had ended in this bare place, where the sand scuffed beneath his sneakers and mostly the dozen motels and tacky seashell shops were not yet open for the season. Across from their motel Arnie found the marina, where rocks had been piled into a jetty that protected a pocket of water from the surf. Some of the boats had giant spools on which their nets were neatly rolled, the sight of which brought Arnie some relief. There were also charter boats with signs that trumpeted the daily rates. Where the land met the dock he found an open bait shop, where he asked for coffee and watched the man pour it from a pot that was sitting on a hot plate.

"Be careful, this'll put hair on your chest," the man said as he popped a lid on the cup.

"It's for my mom."

"Well, it'll put hair on her chest too. Unless she already has some."

Arnie thought then of his mother's chest, sweaty and smooth where the sheet pinched back her breasts. Her auburn hair was peppery at the roots.

"You visiting?"

Arnie shook his head. "We're supposed to be staying here for good." From a rack on the counter, he picked up a handful of packets of sugar and creamer, along with two cherry pies in paper wraps—one for the new guy, one for him. His mother's stomach didn't usually kick in until four o'clock.

"Comes to three forty-seven," the man said. "Let me give you a bag for that." While the man put the coffee and pies in a sack, Arnie noticed the stack of tide tables by the register. A buck fifty apiece. On the front cover it said, "The bigger the dot the better the fishing." He flipped through the pages and saw that today was supposed to be a big-dot day.

"And one of these," he said.

The man nodded. "If you're gonna live on the coast you gotta know when low tide is, right?" Suddenly Arnie realized that they hadn't just come to the end of the earth but another planet where he didn't even know the basic rules of life.

"How come?"

"Weh-yell . . . so you can drive your car on the beach, for one," the man said, handing him his three pennies and the bag.

"Our car's a junker. We barely made it out here."

When he heard it coming out his mouth, Arnie realized that this information was too intimate to be giving to a stranger. But the man just said that having an old car was good. "Then you won't care so much if you lose it when you get stuck and the tide comes up and washes it out to sea."

Arnie felt his jaw drop a little while he considered the possibility. The man behind the counter laughed.

"Don't worry. That only happens to the tourists. You got to start thinking like a local now, since you're here for the duration. Pay attention to the ocean. You got to build up your tolerance for rain."

"It wasn't my idea to come," Arnie said, bunching up the neck of the bag in his fist.

"S'okay," the man assured him. "There's plenty of worse places you could be."

∽

WHEN ARNIE GOT BACK to the motel, the door was locked. He banged and waited, then finally Jay opened the door in his flannel shirt and skivvies. "Hey, whassup," he said. His mother was inside the bathroom, filling the tub. Her voice sounded as if it were coming from a tunnel when she called, "Arnie, you find everything okay?"

Of course he had, so he ignored her. Sometimes she acted like he was an idiot.

To Jay he said, "The man at the store said the steelhead were running." *Running*: the word made Arnie think they had to hurry or else it'd be too late. He considered telling Jay about today having a big dot, to see if Jay would know what he was talking about. It would be a kind of test.

"See? What'd I tell you?"

"So when are we going?"

"Real soon," Jay said, studying the bathroom door. "First your mother and I got to get ourselves cleaned up." He grabbed a towel that was folded on a little shelf above the coat rack.

"I got you a pie for breakfast," Arnie said, pulling the coffee out of the bag.

"Great. I love pie." But Jay set both the coffee and the pie down on top of the motel TV, which was old enough to be a box, and picked up an ashtray instead. "Better warm up your casting arm, Little Man," was the last thing he said before he disappeared inside the bathroom. When he opened the door, for a second Arnie could see the white slope of his mother's back, crouched over the water tap.

He tried the motel TV but now, at midday, found only soap operas and cooking shows. The motel TV sat next to their own set, a thirty-six-incher that Jay had brought in from the car last night so that it wouldn't get stolen. Arnie'd brought in his transforming lizard, and for a while he tried playing with it but soon realized that it was the wrong toy to bring because it did not have any purpose beyond changing from one thing to another. And it could not be the two things it was at once—like you could not have the lizard do battle with the spaceship. Too slow to be constantly changing back and forth.

Last night he'd also brought in the fishing pole, just a cheap Zebco rig, nothing to worry about getting stolen, but still. Its reel was made of plastic and shaped like the nose cone of a rocket. He drew back the drapes and opened the balcony's sliding door. It overlooked the dune behind the motel, which was littered with the random plastic that the last storm had delivered up. He could not see the ocean from here but could hear its pulsing underneath the steadier howling of the wind.

He stepped back inside and slid the door shut, his ears humming in the quiet. He could walk to the beach, but his jacket was still locked in the car, and then he thought about what the man had said: *You got to build up your tolerance for rain.* He searched the pocket of Jay's crumpled jeans but did not find the keys there—he must've had them in his flannel shirt. He thought about knocking on the bathroom door then, but could not bring himself to do it. The two of them would be in the tub, flopping around like seals.

So he sat on his bed, eating his cherry pie and watching a fat man in a chef's hat make something called polenta.

It looked like what prisoners of war would have to eat. Even with the TV on, Arnie could hear Jay's laughter made husky with smoke, the water spattering through it. His mother's laugh reminded him of a vine, tendrils wrapping themselves on anything that would hold.

When he finished eating, what Arnie did was stab a piece of the other pie on the hook of his Zebco. Out on the balcony, he pulled the damp sleeves of his sweatshirt down around his fists. Ten yards off in the dune there was a considerable puddle of rainwater, surrounded by broken glass and one abandoned flip-flop. No fish were leaping from it, not that he could see, but two seagulls seemed very interested in whatever lay beneath the surface: they nosed the water and threw drops over their heads. And if you could drive on the beach here, you might just be able to fish in a puddle. Who could tell how things worked now that they'd come to the end of the earth?

Arnie's first cast bounced off the roof overhang on the balcony. His next landed in the mud below, and failed to attract the seagulls' notice. But on the third cast he was able to make his pie-piece land near the rim of the puddle: the two birds gawked at it for a moment, wondering what it was. Then one pecked gingerly and finally managed to pull a piece of the piece loose. Swallowed. Tried to go back for more. This discovery—that the waxy clod was edible—caused the other bird to turn up the volume of its squawk. The two birds commenced lunging in earnest, one stabbing its beak at the pie-chunk while the other huffed its feathers, and while they were caught up in this game of feints and counter-feints a bigger, whiter gull swooped down and gobbled up the hook.

Once it realized it was snagged, the bird landed, then hopped on the ground for a while with a look of confusion that soon gave way to rage. The bird flapped in the puddle and made the sound *kyee! kyee!* while its beak snapped open and shut. Mud flew as the bird slapped the puddle with its wings: *kyee!* But little by little, the bird wore out its fury, until its beak hung open as if it were panting, its tongue flickering in and out, and when it next hit the apex of one of its hops, Arnie reeled in some line: tick tick tick tick tick. Then the bird hung on the end of the line between bursts of flapping and pendulating from side to side. Arnie was worried that if the bird panicked, the hook would tear out of its mouth, so he reeled with a slow rhythm of pauses and starts: tick tick tick tick. He had this idea that maybe if he could get the bird into the dim light of the motel room, he could hypnotize it somehow. He could hold it under his arm and stroke its throat until it opened up and let him gently remove the hook.

"Easy," he chanted as the bird came closer, growing larger as it did, blotting out a bigger portion of the sky. Tired now, the bird's wings fluttered inefficiently and its pink legs dangled like a puppet's. Slowly, and with just a few feet of line played out between them, Arnie backed into the room, reeling the bird with him.

For a minute the room's carpeted interior seemed to sedate the bird as it stood on what his mother had called the credenza, ratcheting its head like an emperor on a balcony, surveying the crowd. But then the gull caught sight of itself in the mirror and burst into a renewed frenzy. It threw itself against this other bird, knocking over the coffee that was on the motel TV, and, finding no bird there, it tried the other corners of the room, heaving itself against the drapes and toppling a lamp. The room's low ceiling further amplified the bird, until it was as big as an eagle, with a beak the size of a gaffing hook.

Finally the gull came to rest again on the credenza, next to the two TVs, a perch from which it looked at Arnie with its yellow eyes. Its beak had an orange spot that bobbled as the bird swiveled the line in its mouth. Though its look was fierce, Arnie could see its heart beating through the feathers. The skin of its breast quivered underneath the white pelt.

Now he could hear them in the bathroom, the water splashing and the tendrils of her laughter wrapping themselves around her normal breaths. He had never hypnotized anything before, but he knew the trick required a shiny object. He used the earrings his mother had left on the nightstand, which were made from Chinese coins, and he swung one of these before the bird: tick tock tick tock. The bird's gaze followed the coin with a slight movement of its head, suspicious but calmer now. Tick . . . tock . . . tick . . . tock. But when his mother suddenly emitted a shrill noise that sounded as if it had been made with the last air left inside her, the bird broke off its concentration. Before it could start flapping Arnie lunged at it and trapped it in his armpit. When the bird snapped at his fingers, he drove them deep into its mouth, worked loose the barb from the tender throat skin, and teased the hook out.

Then came the best part, when Arnie took the bird out to the balcony and watched it fly off like a braggart, as if this were all part of a plan the bird had itself dreamed up. That's when Jay came out of the bathroom with a towel wrapped around his waist. He had no hair at all on his chest, which supported a sinewy, muscley mass.

"What the hell were you doing out here?" He wasn't angry; his voice sounded distracted, as if he had been sleeping. "Jumping on the bed?"

"Caught a bird," Arnie said, holding up the pinched spot on his thumb where the bird had almost broken the skin. "By accident. I was practicing my cast."

Then his mother came out of the bathroom, wearing Jay's flannel shirt.

"What happened?"

"He caught a bird," Jay said. His mother's grin was more of a stunned than a happy look, as if she'd just been knocked down by a truck.

"A bird, huh?" She looked around the room, picked up what was left of Jay's cherry pie, and licked the filling from its center. "Where's that coffee?" she said.

"The bird knocked it over." He thought his mother would be mad, but she just shrugged as she studied the cup.

"Good thing it wasn't our TV," she said, her mouth full of crust. Then she wandered out onto the balcony, trying to lick a spot of cherry goop on her chin that lay just beyond her tongue's reach.

"See how the magic works?" she hollered, her bare legs reminding him of the white bellies of two fish. "You come to the end of the earth and then you catch a bird." Her face still had the spot of cherry goop, and now it also had that misty look, so Arnie knew what was coming next.

"Hey, c'mere." She spread her arms for him, and from experience he knew it was useless trying to avoid her. She would chase him around the room if she had to, he could run outside but then she would chase him around the parking lot.

So he went out and let her trap him with her damp plaid arms, swinging him gently from side to side. "You catch a bird," she said, rocking him, "and then you set the bird free. It's all part of the plan: movement, stasis. Where else could this have happened?"

Arnie did his best to ignore her. "So when are we going fishing?" he asked Jay, the question muffled against her breasts.

"Soon." Jay had picked up his jeans and was feeling the pockets.

"You said first thing. You promised."

Outside on the balcony, Arnie's mother held him and would not let go. Rocking and rocking.

"He's right, Ray," she said. "A promise is a promise."

"It's Jay," said the new guy, lighting up a cigarette.

DOCTOR VICKS

Funny how you can go your whole life without some-thing, and then one day that very thing starts descend-ing on you in droves. As if suddenly the universe has gotten fed up with your renunciations and has decided to make damn sure that you relent to what it sends.

Take, for example, a vacuum cleaner: maybe you've always made do with the carpet sweeper (not even elec-tric) that your mother handed you like a bayonet when you first headed off to college. Life was simple: you pushed the sweeper, its bristles spun around and ate up all the crumbs. And somehow twenty years go by without your ever feeling any need to upgrade the sweeper . . . until one day when this guy shows up on your front porch, lugging a vacuum with an iron snout and a plaid cloth bag like a bagpipe. He comes bearing the news that you've won a free one-room carpet cleaning, and you're trying to tell him: *Oh, no, Mr. Slyboots, whoever you are, my life's just fine the way it is . . .*

But say he barges in anyway, sticks his foot in the door, as the expression used to go back in the days when people were willing to be more literal. Now the foot in the door is this man's speech: *Don't worry, there's no money up front, no risk.* He's screaking the vacuum down your hall, trying to hunt himself up some carpet, which is difficult, your house being planked in wide pine boards except for in the living room where there's some ugly orange mid-depth shag that you have a fondness for lying on when brooding and so have resisted your husband's rallying against it.

Oh, no, Mr. Slyboots, whoever you are, there's always some kind of risk.

The vacuum guy is short and wide, maybe fifty but a hard-earned fifty, his short-sleeved shirt pee-yellow and fraying, a gray tattoo escaping from each hem. One bicep's got two bird feet clenching a crumpled flag; on the other some runes that you decode as the bottom half of U.S. NAVY. He reminds you of Popeye, especially when single-handedly he attempts to lift the sofa in the middle of the room, and though it's only a joke what you say next—about him being careful not to rupture himself—it makes him puff up like a rooster. Apparently you have insulted him, and in retaliation he hoists a chair as if it were a marshmallow. As if to prove you cannot stop him. Rupture himself indeed!

Before you know it, he's got the cleaning attachment mounted on top of the vacuum's snout and is laying down the foam in stripes, saying, *Now, what would you pay for this kind of cleaning power?* as the foam dries into dust. *What would this kind of cleaning power be worth to you?* It's a question he will not let you off the hook of, until finally you guess, *Four hundred dollars?* just to try the number out. It's the wrong one, though, a number that makes the man squint at you with one eye bugged, as if he wants to punch you. But then he swallows the big gob in his throat and picks up his spiel where he left off, at the part about the Denby Company's installment plan. Five years at only forty-five dollars a month—that's what you'd pay for this kind of cleaning power!

You sit on the stairs, watching the man grunt in the wake of his machine while his whole story assembles inside your brain in flashes. How he did not think it would come down to this, humping vacuums on and off of porches, how he thought his pension was in the bag . . . until downsizing cut him short. And he is humiliated by his day-in, day-out need to proclaim the virtues of the Denby, or it's you on the stairs who imagines that he is, or it's you imagining that you imagine: who can tell when by late afternoon you're always buzzed? When the man squats to adjust the pile-depth feature, and you see the spot where the sole of his black loafer is worn clean through, you resign yourself to doing what you can to save him. Forty-five dollars a month is not much, after all. And cleaning has always held your interest.

∾

ACTUALLY it's the crevices that interest you, the creases on the front door of the stove, for example, where the dirt congeals, combines with grease, and changes form. There it becomes durable to the harshest solvent, a matter stronger than mere dirt. You have to stab it with a knife and pry it out like the old mortar in the stone walls that snake their pathways through these woods.

The idea had not appealed to you at first—your husband's suggestion, then insistent lobbying, that you all move out here to the woods. You all: husband, wife, son. The woods: scrubby forest, logged off long ago. The rationale was that your son had started hooking up with trouble, had committed break-and-entry and been caught. But something about this explanation sounded fishy, sounded like a cover for some other story about what's going on, a story that has to do with you, though you are not sure what it is. *Oh, no, Mr. Slyboots* or the equivalent of which you were about to say, when your husband tricked you by bringing you here to see this house, with its clean plank floors and their umber grain, the intricacies of which you could spend a lifetime studying. And the front porch that overlooked an old mill creek, which flashed by white and silver where it passed over stones, the same round stones whose fellows have been mortared into the foundation upon which the house itself sits. First thing you did was go down to the creek and yell to see how loud a yelling it had the power to drown out, which had embarrassed your husband (beside him the realtor standing on the porch in heels), but he let you do it because he knew it would win you over, another trick.

So now in the morning your husband drives off, a funnel cloud of dry leaves and gravel. Somehow fate has afforded your marriage just one car. (Your husband chalks it up to money, but this is the kind of simple explanation you distrust.) You console yourself with the notion that *stuck* is another way of saying *off the hook*: all day you can let the ghosts tell you the story of every ding in the floor-boards as you wax them down on your hands and knees. Like the ghosts, you would be glad to die here in this noth-ing town: New Woodland, not even a name but a promise of one, a promise of something that has not happened yet. Your husband likes it, you suspect, because the town has no liquor store, no boys wearing baggy jeans and slantwise ballcaps. Therefore he thinks you and your son are safe here. Ha ha ha.

∾

WHAT YOUR SON has done is break into a house, in the company of another boy, with whom he microwaved the telephone and an expensive collection of Hummel figurines. This would have not been so bad—in fact, the idea interested you: how the telephone looked as it melted into itself, as observed by your son peering through the window into the little lighted booth. But the boys also turned on the water taps and left them running, causing thousands of dollars' damage, and so instead you tried to do something stern with your face when you asked him why. Of course, your son merely shrugged, your son being a maestro of the shrug—slowly his shoulders traveled toward his ears, his right one elevated slightly higher and his head cocked in that direction while simultaneously his right eyebrow lifted and his left eye squinched. The movement of the arms lags slightly behind that of the shoulders, the hands led by the meat at the base of the thumb as they rise up, flip over, and come to rest palms up, in the posture of Jesus.

Finally your son said, "Skipper wanted me to do it."

Then the words came to you as if you were dredging up deep silt: "Well, if Skipper wanted you to jump off a bridge, would you do it?" This was what your own mother had said. You remember wondering what the bridge had to do with anything.

Your son considered for a moment, still holding the Jesus pose.

"Sure," he said.

∾

IT DOES NOT MATTER if your place in the world is small: you make the food, you clean the house. You know the only true world is the one you carry inside of you, and what appeals to you about cleaning is the way it gives you hope that this interior world can be perfected—you *can* run a toothpick around the creases in the stove and in this manner attain enlightenment. And it turns out that you are not sorry at all that you bought the Denby (which you hide in the closet, your forty-five-dollar secret). You use its crevice tool between the floorboards, extracting hairs that have lain stretched out for a century, now restored to their natural curl.

The Denby even has a glass-topped reservoir where you can see the ancient crumbs collect, magically, in the shape of the letter *D* (for Denby!). There is an explanation, of course, a metal grid in the shape of the *D* through which the air gets sucked. But to you it is Ouija, inverted: the ghosts bring the letter to you instead of making you discover it. And these are ghosts who have no special fondness for suspense. These are reliable ghosts who'd just as soon have you always end up with the letter *D*.

So there is this to entertain you—seeing the *D* appear again and again. And there is also lying in your upstairs bedroom with a bottle of cough syrup, Doctor Vicks. In the bed pushed against the southern window through which you watch the bigleaf maple leaves light up before they fall, the quilts smell like your mother who died long ago. And there is also putting on your husband's old coat, tramping rubber-booted along the creek with Doctor Vicks a small red man in your pocket. When the wind picks up and makes the limbs click, you can find a place to stand where the birches will accommodate your arms' spread, your head thrown back and your roar drowned by the louder roaring of the creek. So how come everybody thinks it's you and not the creek who's crazy?

∾

YOUR SON WAS BORN only fifteen years ago, and yet you are starting to forget how it was when he was in your body. You remember that the pain grew intense and then you'd begged to be put out: the world went dark for a while and when you woke they handed you a perfect son. And because you were not aware of his leaving, it was easy to forget that he *had* left—sometimes you dreamed him still inside you until you woke to hear him crying. Or crawling around, creaking the floors. Or as he is now: lying on his bed with the headphones on, his body jerking as if it were being zapped by a thousand volts.

But is he not like any other kid? Okay, he has destroyed a house, but he has also promised not to do it again. Hard to tell at this point whether your husband's plan has worked—to bring the boy out to the woods to save him. Sometimes your husband will be standing in your son's bedroom, angrily brandishing a film canister that holds your son's meager stash of pot. Your husband shakes this rattle like a shaman, and your son resists by refusing to take the headphones off, so that he twitches like a zombie on the bed while your husband yells. It's a creepy ceremony, so you stay downstairs when it's going on.

Often at night your son sneaks into the woods. Your husband's idea is to install double deadbolts and hide the key, but you have dreams of fire, the three of you black fetuses crouched before the door. It wouldn't work anyway, for your son can also use the gutters as his means of escape. Sometimes you hear him rattling down the spouts, and then, flashlight in hand, your husband is off chasing him across the lawn. But your son is quick and knows the shortest route to each trailhead. Useless to go after him with a car: he can get anywhere without a road. Out of the three of you, he is the one who's come to love the country best.

Your job is to keep tabs on your son—since, as your husband points out, you're not doing anything anyway— though his suggestions are ridiculous: that you walk your son to school, that you establish a lookout from which you can see him should he leave the schoolyard. Instead, you and your son conspire to indulge each other's silences, and he is grateful. He even shows you the drawings he makes in the margins of his textbooks, cities being devoured by strange machines.

But then one day you betray this trust by following him: at the end of the drive you watch him stuff his muffler in the mailbox. Then he crosses the road and continues down the railroad right-of-way, where another boy is wait- ing. They walk along smoking cigarettes that they hold between their thumb and fingers in an attempt to look like men, though their backpacks are overscaled to their bodies and the sleeves of their plaid jackets fall too low on their hands. The autumn woods are brown and bright as the boys crunch along on the gravel, while fifty yards back you're carefully stepping from tie to tie.

Where the tracks veer over the creek, they walk to the middle of the bridge's rusted trapezoid and sit on the ends of the ties with their legs swinging in the air above the water. The other boy extracts from his pack the bulky object you'd assumed was books: a radio instead. They sit there with their shoulders hunched like the wings of perch- ing hawks, their wrists crossed between their legs, smoke rising from their crotches as they wiggle listlessly to rap music. Sometimes laughter erupts from them: your son's high giggle, the other boy's loud bray. You cannot hear their words except for when one occasionally rises above its brothers: *douche bag* or *chickenshit*. Your son and his friend are so boring that your follicles prickle, and you have no choice but to let your feet go to sleep because the boys might hear you if you stamped them in the gravel.

Finally what they must be waiting for happens: you have to fight the urge to shout, because surely they too can feel the way the tracks begin to sing. Reluctantly, slowly, the other boy gathers his boom box, and he and your son each move to the outside of one of the bridge's I-beams, where he places the radio in the hollow between his feet. Their toes fit inside the beams; the heels of their boots quiver in the air. They hold on with all their might as a dozen freight cars whoosh past. The girders scream like a sawmill as the log runs through it, the boys hugging tight with their long hair blowing behind them in the shape of fans, their teeth gritted and their mouths flaring with the effort of trying not to be blown backward off the bridge.

You cannot breathe until the last car is safely past, whereupon your knees buckle and you clatter to the ground. But the boys can't hear this over their loud whoops and high-five slaps. Eventually, when they pack up the radio and continue down the tracks, you leave them to it: they've worn you out. Later, you will find the wrappers in his pocket and know that they hitchhiked to McDonald's, eight miles away by the interstate. Which is how they celebrate their finding themselves not dead.

❧

so now you could say to your husband: *I know what he's doing, he is waiting for trains to pass over the creek, so he can hold on to the bridge.* Your husband will ask why your son does this, and you will have to tell him that there is no reason. Then of course your husband will protest: *And you didn't stop him? What if he was injured? What if he was killed!* He's right: maternal instinct should have led you to throw your body down on the tracks, the mother bird sacrificing herself. But somehow your son is no longer susceptible to your protection; he's a bird that has already fledged. You see him out there and can almost not remember how it was when he was inside your body. If you were a hawk, he might even be the one you'd eat.

You could try explaining this to your husband, but he has lost patience with your theories: you have quit drinking, you are supposed to be shaping up, no more talking about ghosts or hawks or angels, which in his mind are equally winged, all of them versions of the same thing, namely signs that you are going off. So you keep quiet when at night he sits at his drawing table, thinking onto paper the buildings that will become the city. The city is in good hands, because your husband has unerring taste: it was he who bought the Mission-style antiques that fill the house. Furniture for looking at, the sofa priceless yet spare as a bench. This is why you have held out for the ugly patch of orange shag: something to roll yourself into, something that will accept you without question. And now, with the

Denby, its scalp turns up no crumbs. Clean is your surrender to domestic life; ugly is your protest. Clean but ugly. But clean is your protest too.

∽

AT NIGHT you go driving, for your husband doesn't like to shop. Eight miles away by the north-south interstate, by the McDonald's and the truck stop where the semis squeal, there is also a giant Eurymart where every possible thing gets the chance to gleam as if electricity were pulsing through it. This is only a trick of light, the Saint Elmo's fire of fluorescence, but still it comforts you at midnight to see civilization buzzing—buzzed but yet still orderly, spaced-out but ultra-clean.

Your husband cannot bear the Eurymart because he says the building has no soul. But he is wrong; the problem is that the Eurymart's soul is so big that you have to be willing to let yourself be swallowed by it. The Eurymart makes you manic, giddy; you can lose yourself for hours. Red boxes of laundry soap tower overhead, look up at them and you're liable to swoon. Enough food to stock all the underground bunkers of all the paramilitarists in these hills. You can't just march around with a shopping cart; instead, they give you a sledge you have to tow behind you like a barge. When you polish off your Doctor Vicks you can just buy yourself another—hell, you can buy a dozen bottles, shrink-wrapped together in the family-sized pack.

An elderly gentleman in a yellow Eurymart apron helps

you load into your car this week's teenage-boy-stomach's-worth of food. Afterward, the trunk sags visibly, like a woman whose hips have given birth to many kids. When you try to give the man a dollar his face turns redder in the redness of the taillight glow. No, he says, he can't take tips.

You should go home now, but instead you head south on the interstate, where halfway between the towns of Ethel and Castle Rock there's a sign for a rest stop named Castle Ethel. Here senior citizens with the fortitude of Mongolian nomads dole out coffee through the thick part of the night, night after night, for unfathomable reasons. They want you to tell them your story and are satisfied even if it only concerns what you saw in the Eurymart. In particular they like hearing about the new colors the vegetables come in, yellow tomatoes and purple bell peppers; they like gathering data that proves how strange the world's become. Then they'll let you beg off to use the pay phone on the far side of the parking lot: if there's anything strange about a woman using the pay phone at two a.m., they don't let on. Two a.m. is Castle Ethel's idea of broad daylight.

The pay phone sits on a post beyond which is wilderness, the receiver cable just long enough to reach into the car if you pull up close beside it. And you can sit here in comfort, dialing the sunny places fed by 1-800 lines: Tampa, Scottsdale, the catalogues spread out on your lap. "If my foot is ten inches long and four inches wide, would I take the Sunday Strider in a size eight and a half or nine? And exactly what color is mulberry—are we talking like a raspberry or would you say more of a grape?" It's nice to hear yourself addressed as *Ma'am*. When you want to terminate these conversations, all you have to do is tell them that your credit card is Diners Club.

Or sometimes you call the husband-and-wife TV Jesus team to ask if they'd let you come live on their Florida compound—you've seen the spread in *People* magazine, you know about the private jet. Unrepentant, the wife still wears her Grandpa Munster makeup even though the husband has recently been publicly tarred for leading a circle jerk with some other members of his flock. The members pulling on their members. "It's not a crime, I don't hold it against him," you tell the young voice that answers the phone; still, she will not give you any information until you provide her with an estimate of the dollar value of your net assets.

And only once were you ever frightened there, staring into the forest that skirts Castle Ethel, your Styrofoam cup paused on your lip when suddenly you realized that what you'd thought were two empty skin-colored plastic grocery bags were in fact two sets of limbs intertwined among the shadows. "Gotta go," you told the Jesus person as you leaned way out the window to recradle the phone. For a minute you were quite sure one of the sets of limbs was your son's, tangled inside the plaid coat worn by the other set of limbs. Their hair shone like that of beautiful long-haired dogs while they strained against each other and keened as if bits of glass were running through their bowels.

It was a vision you drove away from as fast as you could, though on the way home you reconsidered: it *could* have been some flesh-tone plastic grocery bags, and an old sleeping bag flapping in the wind; the coat you thought you saw was just its plaid interior and the hair was its nylon shell. You were still mulling it over in your own kitchen at three a.m., unloading the groceries only to discover that once again you had forgotten milk.

∽

THE NIGHT is a tunnel that shrinks as the year draws to a close, contracting to fit inside the circumference of your headlights. Then the world becomes only what the car can itself contain: the radio, the heat, the bottle of cough syrup on the seat beside you like an obedient child.

And if the night is a tunnel, what awaits you at the other end? An opening into light? A wreck? Pulling off at Castle Ethel? Or simply going home? On the road home there's a sign for New Woodland Marsh, a nature sanctuary on the edge of town, which you've driven by who knows how many nights and dawns until on one of them you turn here. Three miles of gravel road that plunges through the gulleys, the fearsome thump and scratch of tree limbs on the roof. At the end a parking lot and a sign that shows the layout of the nature trail, the trail an elevated boardwalk that lets you walk atop the marsh, the dark eroding below you as your boots plunk along the boards.

Eventually it leads to a dry island in the middle of the marsh, where wrens flitter and herons squawk from the highest limbs of the scraggly alders. Oddly enough, you smell the remnant of a fire and realize that you've stumbled into a clearing, a clearing full of frosted stones the color of jewels. Maybe they are hunks of marble. Maybe the trees here were petrified and turned to minerals a million years ago. Then one of the stones shifts and changes shape, and you hear a rustling as if from a lady's ballroom gown. And more of the stones shift, change shape . . . by now you're backing toward the boardwalk again.

It's too late to run: suddenly you're struck by a flashlight beam, and you know now that the moving stones are children wrapped in sleeping bags, a dozen who have spent the night here. One girl calls out, "It's Jason's mother!" and a low singsong wafts your way: *Whoa-oh, Ja-suh-uhn's busted . . . Jay-suh-uhn's busted.* The woods ring with the song while you try to think of an appropriate thing to say, but by the time you can dredge up the words your son has already said them: *What are you doing here?*

∼

CHERRY TONGUE is the giveaway, that fuzzy, red, iridescent tongue whose scent you camouflage by chewing Life Savers. In any case your husband can tell the scent doesn't come from gin. So when he asks, "Have you been drinking?" you can answer him indignantly. He is wrong and he knows it, you have not had a real drink for months. And there *is* a difference: Gin sent you down like a rock kicked off a cliff. Gin was the tall man standing up there while you fell too fast too far for there to be any use in crying out.

But Doctor Vicks you could speak to and he *would* talk back; your head might grow yards from your feet but even then the squat red man was there to look you in the face. Or rather your feet might grow yards from your head, for the feeling was not as if you floated but rather as if you waded through the real, the real having thickened into jelly around your legs. Doctor Vicks engulfed you in a warm swirl like the sweat underneath a man's armpit, which you could curl yourself into. With your husband, this had stopped happening long ago. And sure, you used to love him, but how can you love anyone to whom you are an embarrassment? Next question: are you an embarrassment to your son Jason? Hard to tell. For now, you are two dogs circling each other, using your paws to travel sideways. Knowing that you are not really going anywhere, knowing that you are only headed back to where you were.

∾

THE SUNDOG LADY shows up at the wrong time of year for vacuum sales. Now the rain falls steadily and instead of leaf crumbs what you have is mud against which the Denby is powerless so long as the mud stays in liquid form. So this is what occupies your day: waiting for the mud to dry so that it can be sucked. You haven't the heart to tell the Sundog lady that not two months ago you bought a Denby. Instead you are thinking about all those years with just the carpet sweeper, and now this glut of vacuum salesmen— salespeople. How strange life's feast or famine.

Still, the Sundog lady importunes on you to let her give you a demonstration—"then you'll know what I'm talking about." Brown-skinned and wearing great padded silver boots, the Sundog lady responds to your invitation across the threshold: "Honey, if you don't mind, I think I better get these moonboots off my feet."

Underneath, she's wearing pantyhose, and you walk her quickly to the carpet. You've noticed that she has no vehicle, and she explains that she walked from the crossroads where her husband dropped her off, with the intention of demonstrating—she calls it "demo-ing"—the Sundog along the way. She has the vacuum strapped to a rolling luggage cart with a complicated web of bungee cords that she untangles. Then she shows you how the Sundog has a water reservoir through which the dirt gets sucked, even the mud will be sucked, believe you me. And though you just this morning ran the Denby over the shag carpet, still there's a brown film wobbling on the surface of the water reservoir after she makes one swipe.

It sort of sickens you: how hard you fight the world, how the world keeps coming in.

The Sundog lady sees you frown and understands—and is grateful—that you are genuinely interested and not just letting her go through the motions. She also knows she's got a live one on her hook, and so do you: you could buy a vacuum and spare this woman any further trudging along the shoulder while the cars spray rooster-plumes of mud into her face. You have that power. You are that well off, really: if you were a more reliable sort of wife you'd be sure to have a car. And you could build a fire and let the Sundog woman spend the afternoon in her stockinged feet with a mug of tea. No doubt she would find your husband's furniture odd and sterile: not much there to cushion her meaty bones. Instead the two of you will have to lie on the shag, underneath the old quilts that smell like your dead mother, eating Oreos on salad plates until the light grows dim and she calls her husband to come fetch her.

As she navigates the vacuum around your living room, the woman speaks in the reassuring tones of farther south, those sunny places that you talk to on the phone from Castle Ethel. She's admitting that you are the first person today to let her in. But she does not seem disheartened: "Ain't had the chance to get out in the country much," she says. Because you ask, she offers that it's pretty, but that she would be afraid to be alone out here at night. "Too much space with nothing here," she says, "and I'd always be feeling like it was up to me to fill it up."

REPORT FROM THE TRENCHES

Having never smashed any plates before, I was surprised by their substance, how they made the copper skillets sway on their hooks over the range, jeweling the kitchen with those shards of orange light. Then I wadded the curtains in my fists and threw my weight back against them.

Okay, I'm leaving, Jimmy says. You can take your tit out of the wringer.

Then there's the telltale snarl of his car in retreat, a mufflerlessness out of place in this neighborhood, where the rest of our vehicles were manufactured by the timid Japanese. And then it's quiet, the kind of quiet that's hard work to remember, as I lie in the kitchen, still gripping the curtain rod like a ceremonial sword.

Soon Jill comes in the door that he left open—she's been outside walking her sheltie with all the other neighbors dragging their dogs around until their bowels empty for the night.

You should have shut the blinds, she says. Unless you

really did want everyone to show up here tomorrow with a casserole, she adds.

So what was the fight about this time?

You mean what's the name this time.

Okay, what?

La-riss-a.

She humphs: Now you need to get some holy water and sprinkle it around the house.

Her next bit of advice is that I shouldn't clean up right away: instead I have to spend time basking in the wreckage I've wrought, since in it will appear the phoenix rising from the shards of my old life. But suddenly the phoenix just looks like broken plates, the good set of Spode that belonged to my mother, and when I whack myself with the curtain rod, the dusty curtains are reluctant to part company with the mucus on my chin.

Oh, come on, she says. Name one way that you're not better off without him.

Money, I say finally.

Then Jill digs through the junk mail on the counter and pulls out the credit card applications. Here, she says. Here's plenty of money, and you didn't even have to leave the house.

So we bask for a while, but Jill thinks I'm not trying hard enough, and when she's listened to about as many of my sobs and slobbers as she can stand, she says, Forget it, and starts sweeping up the kitchen. She has to work around the patch of floor where I'm regressing to my fetal self with the Harvey's Bristol Cream. She bends the rod in half and shoves the whole thing—curtains and all—into the garbage. Meanwhile I'm watching her feet from eye-level, the hems of her slacks, her cable-textured trouser socks. And I'm also thinking about how, before she married the old man next door who died and left her with an ample trust, she told me she used to go around robbing mini-marts.

Tell that story again, I say.

Which story?

The one where you're in the car with the boys back East, and the boys have the gun.

She harrumphs a little, says, Why don't you tell it? Since you're the one who's always bringing that old warhorse up.

But I wasn't there.

Jill lets the contents of the dustpan clatter. I wasn't there either, she says. My brain was never in the same time zone as the parts of my body below my neck.

Jill's the only woman my age I know who has a hairstyle that requires curlers—in her sweater and pearls, she could be Lassie's mom. I offer her the bottle, but she insists on making herself a proper drink, her back turned to me, the glassware clinking against the counter.

So you walk into the gas station . . . I say to get her started.

I was never the one who went into the gas station, she corrects. I was always the one who drove.

Okay, I say, you're driving. You're in Amish country and it's midnight. And the boys are in the back seat, bouncing the gun around like a hot potato. They've just come running out of the mini-mart with a big stack of money.

You got it. See? You don't need my help.

Jill stirs her drink with a cocktail fork. An olive floats like a tiny zeppelin between the ice.

That's it? I ask, thinking there must be more to it than that.

That's it.

You're driving?

Hey, I'm driving fast as hell.

She drags a chair over to sit near where I'm curled up on the floor. Jill's sheltie, whose name is Lois, has all this time been lying in the entryway, on the mat that's made of woven weeds. She's been to obedience school, and the way she locks up on command for some reason frightens me. When Jill whistles, the dog instantly unfreezes. Dragging her red leather leash, she trots over to lie against Jill's shins.

So what about when you drive by one of those Amish guys? I ask. One of those Amish guys riding along in a buggy.

You don't worry about them, she says as she reaches down to scratch Lois under the collar. You pass them in the oncoming lane and leave them in the dust.

But what about the horses? Weren't you afraid of scaring the horses and making them bolt in your path?

Jill shrugs. Sometimes you'd look out and straight into the eye of the horse and you could see yourself as you went zooming past. But this would take place in the flash of an instant. And you couldn't really tell if you were just so high you were imagining it.

The kitchen falls quiet again, except for the sound of the baby upstairs on his planet far away, his cries coming in a language that I do not speak. All I can decipher is that he has one idea and that idea concerns rescue, and he knows how to bypass the brain and shoot straight for the glands, producing two wet spots on the front of my blouse that I don't want to think about quite yet. I'm still trying to imagine myself in the car, with the boys and the gun and the money and the horses, and this means stepping out of my whole life.

I think you're going to explode, Jill says, pointing to my shirt.

First tell me how the story ends.

It doesn't end, she says. You use the gun to get the money. You use the money to get the drugs. You use the drugs to get the boys. You use up the drugs and need more money. So you get out the gun and you do it again. It goes on and on and on.

Lois's tail thumps on the floor. Her one idea is *happy happy happy*.

But it ended, I say. I mean, you're here.

I just got old is all, and then Jill laughs. She is, after all, almost thirty.

But here's one thing I remember, she says more brightly. Here's one thing I never will forget. Once we were driving through this tiny town outside of Chambersburg; the only thing this town's got going for it is a pool hall sitting directly across from the courthouse. The boys are in back and they're scared, because tonight for the first time they've had to fire the gun. They had to let the clerk know they were playing for real, so they fired a shot over his head and broke one of the plate-glass windows, which hung for a split second before it fell like a sheet of ice sliding off a barn roof. And then we lit out down the state road, which before long led us through this tiny town, where they've got the speed limit bumped down to twenty-five, only we're cruising through at fifty. And all this time I've been trying to talk the boys down, when suddenly we pass the pool hall with its door flung open on a rectangle of light. It looks sort of like water, and there's this girl standing in it, wearing one of those filmy Amish caps, the ribbons untied and dangling around her breasts. She must have ditched the rest of her Amish gear after she left her parents' house; she's wearing a green dress that's short and slinky, her legs bare underneath—made me wonder why on earth she kept the hat. Something about wanting to flaunt the way all the rest of us think that we're stuck with the cards that we've been dealt, but I don't have time to work it out because I've got to concentrate on driving because suddenly there's cars parked along both sides of the street. There was a guy running his hand up her leg, only I couldn't see the rest of him; everything but the hand was cut off by the doorframe. And she was smoking a cigarette and looking straight at me, like she'd been standing there all her life, waiting for someone like me to come along.

Then suddenly Jill stops talking, her fingers buried in the dog's deep fur. I can hear the baby, my Martian, making the noises that are making me leak. To him I am just a bag of milk, I know this. A giant milk bag, with a pink-brown bull's-eye at its center.

So how does she fit in? I ask, wanting to get back to the girl though it's too late—I know she's gone. My question will only cause Jill to uncross her legs and smooth her wool slacks before taking up the leash.

I just think of her often is all, she says. You were the one who asked.

A GHOST STORY

This happened back in the days when the girl was working as a flagger, which paid ten dollars an hour back when ten dollars an hour was a lot of money, though perhaps the job was damaging what we would now call the girl's "self-esteem"—she'd just graduated from college, she'd not expected that she'd have to stoop to flagging. Which meant standing for hours with a sign in your hand, one side saying STOP and the other SLOW, the same two speeds she saw her life operating in. She wasn't even allowed to make the decision about when to show the STOP and when to show the SLOW; the boss, who mostly stood at the edge of whatever hole they were making, leaning on a shovel, decided that.

It was the kind of job the girl couldn't function in unless she was wasted; she tried a few times and by the end of the day the cartilage inside her knees developed a serrated edge and her arms filled with ball bearings that rattled down against her lungs whenever she lifted the sign above her head. By three o'clock she'd be pounding on the door of the Port-O-Let until whichever of the guys was in there let her in and toked her up. Then suddenly the texture of everything became more vivid; an oily puddle could occupy the better part of an afternoon. And she was proud of the fact that she never killed anyone, though perhaps this was only a matter of luck. Luck and the fact that the girl was willing—whenever she sent people down the road *SLOW* when the sign should have said *STOP*—to throw herself onto the trunks of cars, sounding a *thunk* loud enough to make them halt.

This happened a couple of times, the driver glancing back in terror to discover the flagger girl splayed across his rear windshield. This was how she met the man she dated briefly that summer, who had a convertible in whose tiny jump seat she ended up, screaming, "Look out!" because there was a mail truck approaching the other way.

"Don't worry, I see it," he said. After swerving around the traffic cones while the truck went past, he continued down the street.

"Are you always this hysterical?" he asked, when she finally managed to sit up. She explained to him how she had simply made an error for which she was taking the responsibility by rectifying it herself. Not hysteria but self-reliance. As in Ralph Waldo Emerson.

"We'll go for coffee," he said; then, "No wait a minute, you don't want coffee. What you want is a drink." Yes. The man was nice-enough-looking. He had one of those big mustaches like the good cop in a TV show. So the girl stashed her hard hat and orange vest in the trunk of his

MG while they went for a drink in one of the seedy Chinese restaurants downtown, which were just opening for lunch. She wasn't too worried about leaving the job site—it was a state job and the infraction process was so complex that basically she would have to commit a felony to get the boss to work up sufficient energy to fire her.

And now, after all these years, the girl can't remember much of the dialogue that passed between them. Except that at one point she asked what he did: just filler, a substitute for an actual thought. But he used what she said as a springboard for his own interrogation: "Why is everyone so obsessed with 'do'? Why is it assumed we all need to 'do' something? What exactly do you mean by 'do' anyway?"

She said, "Just forget it."

Then he teased one of her legs off the stalk of the barstool and used it as a lever to spin her around. "Let's just say I'm a househusband," he said. "Without the wife. Without the house." And while she found this slyly sexy, even in the dim of the bar she could tell that the man had used a blow-dryer to style his pepper-colored hair. And in those days blow-drying was a quality she distrusted in men.

But nothing happened: the man simply paid for their drinks and then drove her back to the job site, where the boss grumbled about her explanation—that she'd gone to the emergency room to be checked out after the impact—but did not contest it. "You gotta be the worst flagger girl ever," he said.

A few days later, the man drove by again around quitting time and took her to dinner at a chic French place.

They went dutch, which the girl made a big stink about, though privately she resented his not lobbying harder for the bill. But it must not have been a sufficient degree of resentment to keep her from inviting him home, which in those days was what you did after a date, which you did not call a date. The sex you called "fucking," which was supposed to prove you were a woman who had torn the veils from her eyes. The girl called herself a woman, although the word felt like a thistle in her mouth.

As for the man, he was old enough to be one, with a thicker body than those few college boys whom she'd seen in the buff. And the sex was thicker too when it parked itself atop her like some not-quite-solid mass. She assumed this was one of natural consequences of aging, that the whitewater of sex would slow to a dribble, giving one time to get the adult work of life accomplished—like making grocery lists or calculating the number of days to the next paycheck—while the act itself took place. And when it was done he fell asleep, which the girl counted as an improvement over the college boys too, who afterward would crank up the album *Aqualung* and drop a couple more hits of acid and then want her to come outside with them to toss around the moon-glo Frisbee.

But later, when the darkness was rolling itself back up like a rug, she woke to find the man on top of her again. It was actually not the weight of him that woke her, for he was trying, she could tell, not to disrupt her sleep, but the fact that the room itself was shaking. All she had for a bed was a mattress under which she could feel the floorboards flex.

When the square of frosted glass dropped from the fixture on the ceiling, the man flattened himself on top of her.

"Earthquake," he muttered.

"What are you doing?"

"I was just trying to keep you from being cut."

"No," she said, when the trembling stopped. "I meant before that."

"What? I didn't want to wake you up."

He got up to sweep then, a gesture that she knew was supposed to make her grateful while at the same time giving him an excuse not to have to meet her eyes. And if he *had* asked, he queried as the pile of glass clinked along the floor, wouldn't she have gone along for one more round? Probably, she admitted, but he didn't know that for a fact. In essence, he had raped her.

"Don't be ridiculous. I certainly did not. That was a hundred percent consensual"

"How do you know that?"

He said that it could be inferred from her behavior earlier in the evening. He assumed she'd be willing, and what was the point in her losing sleep over something he could take care of on his own?

Well, fair question, she thought, because what did she know? The girl was not pretty, and she assumed that if she were she'd have more data when it came to men. She was merely young, and when you are young you do not realize the power your youth has, how it trumps everything, even money and smarts and looks. Sometimes (now) she looks at the one snapshot she has of herself from those weeks:

there she is, a waif in a filmy Indian peasant shirt that you can see her nipples through. No wonder she couldn't get any kind of job but flagging. In those days, she went to job interviews like that.

After the earthquake, she was uncertain how she should feel about him. The man was exceedingly cordial, he did not again mount her in her sleep, and there were no after-shocks, the fault held in its new place. Being from L.A., he was not alarmed the way she was, stockpiling a dozen gallons of water in plastic jugs. If it ever happened again, he said she was supposed to dive under a table. "Yeah, right," she said. "If it happens again I'm running." But he swore that she should trust him on this: go for the table.

Even though she came to understand that his ego thrived on his remaining a mystery, little by little, his story couldn't help but leak. And when it did, she felt a few pangs of disappointment pass through her not-so-ample chest, because the story was more mundane than she had hoped. Having to do with windmills. Having to do with his engineering degree and his MBA. Turned out he was trying to start his own company, working on a business plan for putting windmills in the mountain passes. Meanwhile he was living with his baby sister, helping take care of her kids. And this part of his story appeared to be true, at least she saw them. A little boy and girl. They called him Uncle Stan.

On the first weekend they spent together—don't worry, there are only two weekends in this story, it'll be over with soon—he came by with both kids crammed into the jump seat, and they all went roller-skating around the lake. It made the girl happy to mother the children, and the man, she could tell, also took pleasure in her ministrations to them. But as they looped the lake, sometimes when the children weren't looking he reached out and caressed her buttocks. Sometimes he reached farther in, past her buttocks, in between her legs.

When they dropped the kids off at the sister's house, the sister was friendly enough but the girl didn't know what to make of the way the sister held her thin smile just a bit too long in place. Maybe it was pity for her, the girl who was sleeping with her brother without even realizing that he was a ghost. She could tell it was a running joke when the sister called after the kids as they tromped into the house, "Did you take good care of your uncle Stan?"

Then the second weekend they took the ferry to Canada and headed west along Vancouver Island's tip, the sun making the tongues of surf look silver where they lapped on the shore. He drove while the girl rolled from his stash of good Humboldt County weed, the MG's top down, the girl holding the joint up to his lips. Where the road dipped close to beach, they stopped and clambered down the rocks. There the girl squatted behind a clump of grass to put on her two-piece bathing suit (this is what astounds her now, this idea of her in a bikini) and went running down the sand while the man watched her getting smaller as she receded. That's how she pictured herself, in terms of how she looked to him, and on her return she made a point of arcing her legs, her impossibly thin legs that she tried to make look graceful and fluid, hyper-real.

He knew of a bed-and-breakfast on the outskirts of some obscure fishing town, a cabin that sat in the side yard of someone's house, perched on a bluff that dropped to the Strait of Juan de Fuca. There was a hibachi on the deck, and they drove into town for charcoal and red wine and steak, which the man grilled along with thick slabs of potato. Not having steak knives, they had to tear the meat with their teeth, their hands gripping the rind of fat. Afterward, he took her (what a bizarre expression, "took her") as she bent over a chair while he stood watching in the bureau mirror. And when, under their collective weight, the legs of the chair inched apart and sheared off, they continued while she lay facedown on the pile of spindles in the narrow space afoot the bed.

"Hair of the dog," he said in the morning, uncorking another bottle. The owner's practice was to leave breakfast outside the door on a tray, rapping lightly to let the guests know it had been delivered. The girl opened the door with the hem of her T-shirt yanked down in her fist, and the owner, having paused in her retreat to inspect the flower boxes along the drive, made a sour face when she glimpsed the girl's outstanding disarray.

The weather had changed sometime in the night, and the ocean vista that had been so brilliant was packed now with gray vapors. By the time they finished their eggs, the drizzle had escalated into full-blown rain, so they played backgammon and got drunk on the complimentary sherry, draining the decanter while the day grew fuzzy on their tongues. To make something memorable of it, they played out the marquis and the maiden, the stupendous groupie in the bathtub, Margaret-Trudeau-not-wearing-any-underpants-when-she-meets-Leonid-Brezhnev, etc. He lapped the last of the sherry off her chest while she strained at the sheet he'd torn in strips to bind her, though the straining was largely a charade. In fact her tethers were loose enough that as soon as he finished the girl worked herself free.

"You liked it," he said. And she thought: Okay, so she liked it, so what? Is it so wrong to be twenty-three years old and to want a man to ravish you in a strange room by the sea? She wanted many things that she was too ashamed to say.

Then he gathered the hair at the base of her neck and pulled tight enough to bare her throat. "And how about if you'd known I'd spent some time in jail, huh? Some women are attracted to men who've been hauled in once or twice."

The girl was thinking of the college boys she'd known when she asked what for. Chaining themselves to things in protest or growing marijuana in the woods.

"Aggravated assault," he answered, looking away, letting her hair drop.

The girl figured he wouldn't have started if this were not a moment that he took some relish in arriving at with women, this cathartic moment of his getting the story out. Turned out it was a former girlfriend, with a subplot involving her waving around a kitchen knife. Of course, aggravated assault was just the plea deal he agreed to, and she didn't need him to explain what aggravated assault turned into when you decoded it backward through the courts. She didn't say the word, but she did ask why he pled guilty.

"She was the one who'd come over, drunk out of her skull. She was the one who sucked my dick, but how do you prove that?"

The girl didn't know what to say after this; to suggest another game of backgammon seemed like a backward step. More wine appeared to be the only option, more dope to unravel the seam that he'd just stitched. They slept for a while, and when they woke the rain had slacked. So they stumbled down the trail to the beach, just because the beach was there and they were paying for it to be there and had not felt it underfoot.

Way down below, a small cove scalloped into the woods, hemmed by a mound of driftwood that the ocean had tossed up. There were only a few houses whose windows glinted atop the bluff, so they took off their jeans and waded in until their legs began to buckle from the cold. Then the man staggered off to sit with his back against a rock, and with his legs outstretched and his jeans hanging like a stole around his neck he hollered for her to come get on top. When she did, she could hear the crunch of shells beneath him, and their sharp edges egged her on—she wanted the shells to make little cuts on the backs of his legs, so he would see them in the mirror tomorrow and know for sure that they were real. That she was real. She did not want to be a ghost.

"I thought so," he said when they were finished, him sitting there in the lee of the rock looking humpbacked and old, his underwear snagged around one knee.

"You thought what?"

"What I told you. It did turn you on."

The girl thought about saying no, then she thought about saying yes, before striking what she thought would be an enigmatic pose. But the spell she was attempting to cast was undermined by a strong scent, which these two in their theatrics had not noticed. On the other side of the rock they found a dead dolphin, its black and white markings too stark to be real, its eyehole full of flies.

By the time they limped back up the trail, sand spackling the wet between the girl's legs, the owner of the bed-and-breakfast was waiting for them at the cabin. Checkout time was an hour ago, she said in her tight-lipped Anglo-Canadian brogue. Quickly they cleaned the room as best they could, stuffing the broken chair and torn sheets and bottles and greasy bones under the bed, before stopping at the main house to settle up. The man paid with a credit card that was in his brother-in-law's name, and when the girl asked about this as they sped back toward the ferry, he said that his brother-in-law was just doing him a favor because he'd been bankrupt and couldn't get his own credit.

Then he laughed at the wrinkled expression on the girl's face, told her not to get her panties in a knot. Bankruptcy was just another rite of passage, like getting married and divorced. "And I bet you haven't experienced those yet either," he said. "Just wait a few years. Your disaster machinery's barely had the chance to get itself warmed up."

∾

STANFORD STRICKLAND, that was his name, a name with the ring of a movie star from the forties. Or a famous highbrow murderer who has all but been forgotten. I could tell my mother was reading it off a small scribbled sheet when she phoned the other day to say that a man with this name was trying to get in touch with me.

"I know it's none of my business, but he sounded . . . I don't know . . . kind of funny."

"Funny" is my mother's word for any kind of fucked-up, her manners too delicate to have ever allowed her to call attention to my glassy eyes or musty breath. What does it matter, she would argue, when that girl I was is all water under the bridge, a bridge that she has seen me dismantle piece by piece? After the flagging, there came a winter of waitressing that cured me. By the next fall I was enrolled in law school, which was what she'd been telling me to do all along.

Still, she recited the number slowly: whenever circumstances force her to revisit my youth against her will, she likes to draw the details out to make me squirm. By the time she was finished, the line between us glowed red-hot, and I made sure she heard me crumpling my transcription, seconds after I wrote it down.

"I didn't think you'd want it," she remarked offhandedly. "He was the one who kept insisting that I pass it on."

This is the kind of warfare waged by ghosts, these ghosts from whom there is no durable escape. Years later, even if you've gone to the trouble of covering your tracks, they will remember the name of your hometown and call your mother up. If they're feeling especially vengeful in their oblivion, they might even try to describe for her what you looked like all those years ago when they had you tied to that bed. And while sometimes you can banish the physical vessels in which these ghosts travel, the psychic border skirmishes will continue on forever. To mark the boundary between you and them, there will always be a dotted, provisional line.

And then there is also the matter of the border itself, the literal border across which we fled. The first crossing of it had made everything glitter, as if we were snakes with new clear eyes, having peeled off our old skins. But the drive back seemed only oppressive and dreary, the sea walled off by fog. And the surf that had aroused us with its persistent violent crash now sounded unbearably repetitious, like the person sitting next to you on the bus with a hacking cough.

At the ferry dock, they steered us into a gated area where the tarmac was marked off into lanes. We waited there while the customs officers came through, asking the usual questions concerning fruit. The officer who approached the MG was a stout matron about his age, how funny that a woman his age turns into a matron, her breasts large in her white blouse. As soon as she took one look at him in his wraparound sunglasses, it was as if she knew. She *knew*, goddammit. And she waved our car over into the special parking strip, where our bags were taken from the trunk and searched. They found the last bit of pot wrapped in one of his dirty socks.

My bag was clean, though, and the one last favor he did

for me before we parted company forever and for good was to say that I didn't really know him. I didn't know him at all. I was a girl he'd just met in the bar of a Chinese restaurant; he was giving me a ride home because my boyfriend had left me stranded after we'd had a lover's spat. And what with the age difference between us, the enormous volume of my tears, they let me cross.

The whole trip back I stood outside on the deck, watching the birds that floated on the water, which was gray and still and dimpled by rain. I was supposed to call his sister as soon as I got back to the States, but instead, when I reached the ferry terminal on the other side, I hitchhiked home.

And I didn't see him again in town, even though, being the flagger, I saw everyone eventually. For weeks, whenever we started work at a new site the first thing I did was scope out some bushes into which I could dive should he come driving through. But he never did, and when I tried to make sense of it, the only explanation I could get anywhere with was that he had to be a ghost. He was like the phantom that appears in those hitchhiker/truck driver stories, where depending on the version either the hitcher or the trucker has died a long time ago and yet there's this one piece of evidence left behind to prove the visitation. A jacket, say. A baseball cap. Don't think I am insensitive to the irony that my mother is the only person who could back me now about the fact of his existence.

(But on second thought, I know she wouldn't. In a clipped voice she'd say: "Is this really a matter on which we want to dwell?")

What the man left behind was the last shot left on an old roll of film that I had in my camera, taken on our way over on the ferry, when we were smiling and the sun was beaming on our heads. I'm the one who's braless, wearing the indecent peasant smock: a yard of see-through cotton with elephants embroidered on the yoke. He's got his arm around me, he's wearing his shades, his head tilted over mine. And even though I'm the one in the filmy shirt, if you look close enough you can see that in fact he's the one who's insubstantial, as if at any moment he might turn into smoke. And when he does, I'll make a ninety-degree turn and walk right through him. And my solidness will churn whatever's left of him to wisps.

CAVALCADE OF THE OLD WEST

Though the two sisters had grown apart over the years, one routine they kept up from childhood was going together to the little fair that lodged itself for one week every August between the warehouses and the bay. The fair was nothing to write home about: curly fries, Ferris wheel, carny boys with broken teeth. But when they were kids there had also been a hootchie-cootchie tent and a show called Cavalcade of the Old West, which held on through all the years of the girls' growing up, until the times changed.

The Old West included Snoguish the Indian, who wore a fancy bustle made of eagle feathers, and a blind woman in buckskin named Bull's-Eye Vi, who shot at targets with the aid of a mynah bird. The bird squawked out directions: left, right, up, down. Also appearing was Left-Hand Zach the Lumberjack, who'd been maimed in a logging accident and wielded an ax with the one arm he had left. Sampan the Chinaman juggled railroad spikes that were rubbed with petro gel and set aflame. And Leroy the Salmon Boy. What Leroy did was smoke.

Because Stella was older, she put herself in charge, and her practice of fair-going as it evolved over the years led her to hold off on the Old West until the tail end of the night. First she made Ginny prove that she could ride the Hammer without throwing up, after eating a whole caramel apple, seeds and all. Then it was on to games of chance, where Stella stole softballs out of the bushel baskets and fired them at the pyramids of fuzzy clowns while the carny screamed whatever obscenities were in circulation that year until Stella ran off with Ginny in tow. They were girls then, nimble and skinny, skinny enough to slip through the narrow spaces between the stalls. Behind the stalls, they trotted along the timbers that edged the wharf. Stella would kick off her flip-flops, the pads of her feet growing black with creosote. She laughed at the way Ginny flinched when the herons screeched and flew up beside them from the mudflat.

At the wharf's north end, they came up against the back side of the hootchie-cootchie tent, where the girls dropped off the wharf to stand on the riprap piled below, so that their eyes would be level with the tent's bottom edge, which Stella lifted. Inside, the hootchie-cootchie ladies wore filmy gowns that Stella called *nugleejees*.

"That means nightgown in French," she explained.

The ladies paraded around while the barker made embarrassing claims about their bodies: *If she gets up running and comes to a stop, she'll jiggle like a bowl of jelly.* The women giggled, but the girls could tell that their laughter was fake, and not because they were being wounded, no— they were only bored.

And it was from within the cocoon of their boredom that they took off their nugleejees, one by one. Though the promise made out front was that the men who paid to come inside would get to see the women naked, Stella had already clued Ginny in on the fact that this was just a trick. Under the filmy gowns the women wore two-piece bathing suits made of spangly iridescent satin, with scarves attached that were also tethered to their wrists. Whenever a man tried to touch them, the women would use the scarves like dental floss, slicing between their bodies and his hand, drawing the arm away with the scarf, as though the scarf were a kind of net.

Sooner or later the girls would be spotted peeking under the tent, and the barker would kick their heads just hard enough to drive them off. By this time it would be late enough that Stella would permit them to go to the Old West.

One time they got there just in time to see the mynah bird go wild, the blind woman chasing it by following its squawks. The Indian stood, impassive, at the edge of the stage, while the mynah bird lunged in his direction, apparently recognizing its distant cousin in the wheel of ragged feathers that the Indian wore on his butt. And the one-armed logger was no help, drunk and goading the bird with the stub end of his ax.

But Stella's fixation lay with the Salmon boy, who throughout the pandemonium just sat there and smiled, swaying a little, adjusting the plane of his face until his heavy glasses caught the light and sparked. He was, in fact, an armless, legless black man of indeterminate years, who wore a green satin shirt modified to make the stumps of his arms look like fins. His act consisted of his rolling a cigarette in the trough between his nose and lip, lighting it by curling one stalk from the matchbook backward onto the flint.

Like the rest of the crowd, Ginny drowned her horror in polite applause when at last the gray plumes shot from his nose. Over the PA there'd come a blast of scratchy trumpet as he smoked. Then everyone beat a quick retreat—everyone, that is, except for Stella. Leroy would bow for her for as long as she was willing to clap, until the barker told her to get lost.

That was when they were young, of course, because in later years Leroy was gone, and not just Leroy but all the denizens of the Old West, who became "the disabled" or "Asian-Americans" or "First Peoples" and were moved on, fobbed off, put away, somewhere else. And in this renovation the hootchie-cootchie women were also driven underground. Ginny imagined them wandering the rainy streets—in their nugleejees, like wet moths.

～

THE OLD WEST was replaced by various booths that urged civic improvement. In the new West, everyone recycled their newspapers and cans. The water district gave out low-flow inserts for people's showerheads and the city demonstrated the newest in compost bins. Even the wildlife department came with brochures about the perils of DDT and a few mangy birds of prey, to which Stella shrieked, "Kaw! Kaw!" until the young woman on duty told her that if she was going to annoy the birds she'd have to go away.

Ginny always insisted on being the one who drove because the fair, especially the fair, had a way of pumping Stella full of the black humors that made her manic and angry all at once. "Running on hi-test" was how Stella referred to these moods, which Stella traced back to Leroy but which Ginny suspected had more to do with the likelihood of her running into one of her ex-husbands. Sometimes it seemed that the fair existed just to give her husbands an excuse to knock each other around. More often than not, by the time the sky approached its purest dark, and the kids in safety-patrol bandoliers came through swinging their flashlights to herd the crowd home, one of the husbands would be towing Stella toward the car. Then Ginny would have to drive home while the two of them grappled in the back seat. Whenever a car pulled up behind, their bodies would flash as if a strobe light had hit them, lighting Ginny's rearview mirror. They'd be engaged in some exotic form of either sex or warfare, but Ginny had long ago run out of patience with her sister to care which.

The next time Stella called, she'd sound contrite, though she would feign ignorance about the cause of Ginny's hurt. What she said was always a variant of: "I mean, I'd understand if it weren't my husband."

"You mean your ex-husband," Ginny says.

"That makes a difference?"

"You have many ex-husbands, Stell."

"Several. You're resorting to hyperbole."

"Then I'm sure you could tell me which one it was," Ginny says, hating the schoolteacher (which she is, which she'd become) that she could not jettison from her voice.

"Stell?"

"Okayokay." This is Stella's standard apology. "Whatever it is that I don't remember I did, I promise never to do it again unless I don't know what I'm doing when I do it."

∿

THE OLD WEST lasted until the girls were teens, by which time Stella had taken to carrying a flask in her embroidered shoulder bag that was spangled with tiny mirrors. Whatever was in the flask made Stella hoot and holler:

"Bring on the fish boy!"

"Let's have Leroy!"

"Let's see him roll that cigarette!"

And when he was wheeled into the stage's brighter lights, she applauded more wildly and stamped her feet. She was wearing a skirt that she'd made from an old pair of jeans, the hem frayed, barely reaching the top of the V of her legs. It was that time of evening when the bay flattened its surface and turned silver, the last trace of sunlight mixed with the first trace of moonlight to create a dusty paste.

Ginny was eleven that first year of the flask, with only

a vague idea what *drunk* meant. But the word was juicy enough to make the stardust cling to her sister's body, which seemed full of a mysterious sap that garbled her words and caused a few strands of her dark hair to stick to the corners of her mouth. Then she started shimmying, in more or less one spot, while Leroy grubbed his lips through his tobacco. In a kazoo voice she sang, *I'll be your hootchie-cootchie girl, you'll be the jelly man*, while her arms swung and her fingers snapped.

"That girl's out of control," said a woman in the crowd as she looked around for someone in a position of authority. But under their breath the men sucked their teeth and whispered, *Oh, baby*, and *Come to papa*, as Stella shook the new round breasts that had snuck up on her so quickly that she did not even seem aware of them yet.

"Come on," Ginny said, touching her sister, but Stella shook loose.

"I'm not out of control. I know exactly what I'm doing."

Ginny tried to stand so as to block everybody's view of her sister. "So what are you doing?" she asked under her breath. Stella was pedaling her arms and wobbling her hips, submerged in the sweet liquor that filled her, swimming through it with her eyes closed and her breath held.

"Dancing," she said, without coming up.

∽

WHAT HAPPENED in the years that came after the end of the Old West was that Stella dropped out of high school, messed around for a while, then took the GED and ended up getting out of college with a degree in accounting before the rest of her class, facts that she recited often and with a quack of glee. She liked to make up jokes at the expense of other members of her profession, like: How many accountants does it take to screw in a lightbulb? (Answer: none, because they make the receptionist do it so that when she climbs up the stepladder they can all look up her skirt.) She said the reason she chose accounting was because it did not require any thinking that could not be performed by a machine. "Like, six plus seven's thrown me ever since the great brain cell die-off of the eighties, and you know what? It doesn't matter anymore. They've got software that can compensate."

And in this manner Stella won—rich men came to her with their receipts, and she owned a number of good wool suits that she now wore to work. But for the fair her short skirts were still made of denim, though store-bought now and finished at the hem. She liked to wear them with flashy heels in colors whose names Ginny remembered from the big crayon box: fuchsia, celadon, cerise. She also wore sunglasses, an extra pair of which she once tried offering to Ginny: "So you won't be afraid of running into any of your kids or their parents," she said. "Just in case you decide you wanted to cut loose."

"When have you ever known me to cut loose?"

"Hey, Gin, I figure there's a first time for everything."

Ginny made the comment that she was not the sister who usually needed a disguise, but this made Stella shake her head. "No, you don't need a disguise when people see you wearing one every day. Get me out of a suit and no one has a clue."

"I was thinking more about your husbands."

"Oh, them." Stella waved her hand in front of her face as though she were shooing away a cloud of gnats. "They already have their ideas about me."

∾

THAT WAS HOW the Old West ended, that night Stella did her song and dance: *I'll be your hootchie-cootchie girl, you'll be the jelly man.* After everyone scurried away it was just Leroy on the stage, puffing his cigarette while Stella whooped. The barker rolled his eyes. "It's that girl again. Your number one fan."

Leroy squinted and tilted his heavy glasses before he said, "Let's have a look." Then he made the barker push him down the ramp, so that he was there with the sisters on the wharf, peering up at them through his thick lenses. He looked at Stella, then Ginny, then back to Stella again.

"That's what I call groceries," he said.

Up close, Ginny could see that his shirt was cheap and crudely stitched. When Stella asked if he wanted something to drink, he scratched his shoulder against his chin, which had a few black hairs too sparse to qualify as a beard.

"I s'pose I could do with a Coke," he said.

Ginny was dispatched to get it from the concession stand at the other end of the wharf. And while she waited in line, the evening dimmed—by the time she was headed back toward Stella with the cup in her hand, the bay was more black than silver where it stretched across the opening between stalls opposite the Old West's stage. Farther north, on the other side of the bay, sat the pulp mill lit up like a steamship, its stacks churning out the vapors that reduced everyone who ventured down to the waterfront in those days to tears.

She could not find Stella at first—she was not where Ginny'd left her—though eventually she spotted the wheelchair tucked behind the skee-ball booths and a shooting gallery. Stella was sitting slantwise on Leroy's lap, her white shirt hanging on the back of the wheelchair, where it fluttered like a flag. Ginny knew that her sister was the one who'd done the unbuttoning, the Salmon Boy's fingers sealed inside his fins.

"Whoa. Double trouble," he said when Ginny approached. But Stella was only annoyed.

"What are you looking at?" she snapped.

∾

"OH, THAT WAS YEARS AGO," Stella says, waving her hand across her face, again the gnats. She has her bare feet on the dashboard; she's using the earstick of her sunglasses to dig mud from between her toes. The reason for the mud is that at around ten o'clock Stella had grown annoyed at the way her heels kept getting stuck in the cracks between the planks. And she'd flung her shoes off the wharf, hollering after them, "To hell with you!"

That's all it was: a woman standing with one leg crossed behind the other to peel the shoe off of her heel. Then other leg/other shoe. Then they both get fired into the drink.

That's all it was, a woman taking off her shoes and flinging them into the sea, and yet seeing this somehow made Ginny forget (for a minute) all her sister's petty offenses throughout the years—after all, wasn't Stella right, weren't her transgressions petty? So that what remained was everything about the fair that did not change: the cotton candy like cheap pink wigs and the smell of frying onions, the boys with giant stuffed animals on their shoulders that they'd won for their beloveds, though the conquest had cost them a hundred bucks.

"Hey," Stella says, "you know why accountants always want to meet girls they can bring home to their mothers?"

"Why?"

Stella stops digging to look up at Ginny. "Guess."

"I give up."

"You always give up."

"Just tell me."

Stella wipes the earstick on the dash before popping the sunglasses back on her face. "Maybe I don't feel like it anymore," she says sulkily as they idle in the car, waiting for the traffic to clear from the parking lot.

"Here's the difference between you and me," Stella says at last. "You'd be embarrassed if you were me, but I'm not.

Even when I was a kid, I knew exactly what I was doing. When I'm ninety years old and peeing in a bedpan, that night with Leroy'll be how you remember me and don't tell me it won't. When it comes to you, I'll be fourteen forever. And how much would other people give for that, unh? To be fourteen forever? If I could bottle that, I'd make a mint."

Ginny doesn't answer because she's still thinking about her sister's shoes, ebbing in the Sound, bright red. Meanwhile, Stella takes the flask from her expensive leather Coach bag and drains the last swig, the flask being another thing that hasn't changed, though she keeps better booze inside it these days.

"Anyway," Stella continues, wiping her lips with the back of her hand, "that's why you always come back here with me, though I'm bound to drive you nuts. There's always a chance that I'll be able to come up with something that'll top having my tits licked by the Salmon Boy. I don't think so, but you never know. Maybe someday that old Indian will reappear and you'll catch me balling him. Or the blind lady!" she quacked.

Then there's quiet in the car for a while. "So what's the answer?" Ginny says.

"Answer to what?"

"The girls and the accountants and their mothers." But Ginny can tell that Stella is already bored by the accountants.

"Hunh," she grunts. "The answer is: because they still live with them. But see, it's not funny anymore. That's what happens when you give up. All the funny goes away."

By now the traffic has filed out of the parking lot, and

when Ginny pulls out, the fair lights in the side-view mirror blur into one smear. They're headed north along the shore road, though this is not the direction home. Ginny's just glad to be driving with no husbands, with her sister in the front seat.

"So where are your husbands tonight, Stell?" she asks, and when Stella says, "Who?" in a rednecky voice, Ginny can't help but laugh.

"They're history, Gin. I swear sometimes I can't even remember their names." Then Stella sticks her head out the window and shouts *Leroy!* to the night.

"Isn't it strange?" she says when she pulls in her head. "That someone you love can dry up and blow away like an old leaf? Whereas ten minutes with the Salmon Boy is something that I never will forget."

They've come out of the trees, and here the house lights shine on the bay's far shore, marking the contours of the hills. The far shore is also where the mill sat, lit up like a steamer the girls once claimed someday would carry them away. When they were girls, in the pulp mill days, the air smelled so sour that a whiff of it would bring tears to your face. But it's been years since the pulp mill burned, and now the air tastes clear and sweet.

HOUSE OF GRASS

Before Yvonne Beauchemin made her final exit, she had a vast spread catered for us her neighbors by the best (and as it happens the only) French restaurant in town. First let me get the end of the story out of the way, for I am no lover of suspense: she did herself in the next day in her Peugeot, in a pigskin coat worn inside out. Her coat pocket contained a note, unsentimental and succinct, to the effect that she wished her ashes to be spread here on the Puget Sound.

No, we were not intimates. I know these things only because I was the one who found her, early morning, while taking my daily constitutional around the labyrinthine drive of our housing development, which is called Infinite Vistas. Let me also explain that to purchase a home at Infinite Vistas one must be at least sixty years of age, and suicide among our ranks is not uncommon. Anticipating this, the builders took care not to provide us with garages. Instead we have carports, under which Yvonne Beauchemin attached a length of dryer duct to her tailpipe. The hose ran on the far side of the car and was not visible from a distance, but when I came closer, I saw that the carbon monoxide had already done its work and turned her skin the color of a red plum.

So there you have it. As I've said, it's a common enough local tragedy. Sooner or later those of us who are not lucky enough to drop neatly dead will contract painful and wasting illnesses that we fear will force us to beg our children to put us out of misery. Do I sound heartless if I say that we've trained ourselves not to grieve overmuch?

When she first came to me wanting pills, she knew exactly what to ask for, having read the book. Here at Infinite Vistas we've all read the book; we know which pharmaceuticals would shuffle off our mortal coils. You can imagine the burdens of being a medical man in a community like this, how it forces one to duck his head, to do his walking at an hour inhospitable to other souls. In Yvonne Beauchemin's case, I felt especially culpable for being the GP who'd first sent her shuttling up the pike, from internist to oncologist to surgeon and back. Sometimes I wonder what good I have done, when a person walks in complaining of something so minor as a stomachache and I have to tell him or her as the case may be that no, it's not simple at all: you're dying. And it seems as if my words more than anything make it so.

Some months after her last surgery, she was again sitting in my office, a small brocade cap like an African king's drawn down on her head. She had jeans on, the silly paper cape over her breasts but by this time I could tell Yvonne Beauchemin had no patience for petty embarrassments.

"Henry," she said in her wet Swiss vowels. "I'm having trouble sleeping. Be a good fellow and write me a scrip for Nembutal." Because her long-dead husband had also been a doctor of some sort, a psychiatrist I think, she knew how to get her tongue around a word like *scrip*.

"You wouldn't get caught," she insisted.

"It's not a matter of caught."

"Oh, come on, Henry . . . I bet you wouldn't even have to write the prescription, now, would you? I bet you've got enough squirreled away in your own medicine cabinet at home."

She was right, of course: I did have my own dozen tablets. And not just my dozen but dozens more, enough to kill all of us here at Infinite Vistas. This was the problem: if I gave them to Yvonne Beauchemin there would be no end to the dying neighbors I would see.

"You're afraid," she said then, and I agreed that this was so.

After she'd sat and stewed for a while, she said, "Okay, forget I asked. As they say in the spy books: we never had this conversation. There's plenty of other Nembutal in the world."

"Breathe," I said, and she breathed, though there was an ominous rustling to it, as if her lungs were full of dried-up leaves.

∾

INFINITE VISTAS—or IV, as we like to call it, and it's hard to see how the builders could not have anticipated our obvious jokes—is the kind of gated community that women with money move to after their husbands die, a pretzel arrangement of small overpriced homes laid out with views of the water, where for an immodest monthly fee one will never have to attend to the physical work of living. We moved here when my own wife was ill, because of the roll-in entries and the paddle door handles. "A place where you can be on death's door and still get it open yourself," my wife liked to quip. She was, as they say, a trouper.

Yvonne Beauchemin's house sat on the opposite side of our cul-de-sac, a stand of manicured firs between us. I suspect the place appealed to her only as an easy place to land between her frequent travels, because her own needs were few. When she was well she used to climb up onto the roof of her carport to hose the leaves off, her body as lithe as a girl's as she stepped from the ladder's shimmying peak. By day she wore exercise clothes, not the kind for aerobics at the club but rather those sold at the mountaineering shop in town—expensive windbreakers and nylon pants. She was not, however, the kind of woman whom I could see engaged in any sport that would make her sweat. Instead she kept chained under her carport a yellow kayak that in the early mornings I'd sometimes come upon her sliding onto the Peugeot's roof. And I learned not to offer help, for the first time I did she fended me off.

"This is how I work my upper body," she said, shooting the boat onto the roof rack with one heave. Then she turned and offered me her biceps. "Feel that, Dr. Henry. Is that the arm of a little old lady?"

Impressed, I exaggerated enough to say that I believed she could out-arm-wrestle my grandson, who was at that time on the high school football team. I told her that he also had a kayak.

"You'll have to have him come out and paddle with me," she said as she tightened the straps on her roof rack. When she was through, she turned to me and winked.

"Don't worry. I only take lovers who've reached the age of legal consent." She hopped in her Peugeot and gave me a wave, but as she was driving away, she rolled down her window to say one more thing:

"Though you know, Dr. Henry, how much it varies from state to state . . ."

∾

IN THE INTEREST of family togetherness I once tried to share my grandson's enthusiasm for the water. But I came to the conclusion that being trapped for hours in a precarious plastic craft in which urination is impossible is no sport for me. Weak bladders and decaying lower backs have caused most of the residents of Infinite Vistas, which has its own boat ramp, to forsake paddling in favor of small-horsepower motors and trailers that can do the lifting in and out.

But being prone to seasickness, I took up bird-watching instead, to feel that I was at least getting my money's worth out of the premium we pay for being on the water. Something besides work that would take me from the house, though not for too long—I needed just a short spell from the bedside. And beauty too, I must admit that I was impelled by beauty, in a life that at that time surrounded me with all the body's ugly exudates. The perfection of birds is like that of no other mortal thing—their sheen, their obsessive grooming. You never see them get scraggly until the bitter end, and even then it seems that it is the eclipse of their loveliness that kills them more than any underlying disease.

In winter, when ducks fill up our bay, there is a period when as often as not on my trips to the boat ramp I'll find at least one hooded merganser. Perhaps this is a bird you do not know, a duck with a more intricately chiseled beak than your standard mallard's, broad at its base, then tapering to a stalk that ends in a pointed droop. The body is tawny on its sides, the stark white breast bordered by two black stripes, the delicate head concealing a crest that can inflate to show a white polygon outlined in black, one corner set behind the yellow eye and flaring at the nape. What mesmerizes me is how it looks like a mosaic built from three completely different animals: the crest of a lizard, the flanks of a fox, the stripes of a zebra. And maybe it's just in my estimation that this seabird appears more skittish than most, being never quite sure what it is.

Of course, there were also the strange clown-faced scoters, and the cormorants that unfurl their iridescent blue wings in the sunlight and stay poised that way as if they were fashioned out of metal. At home, I was medicating my wife far beyond what was deemed reasonable five years ago. Pain was the medium in which she floated, no cure for that, but still I was determined to glaze its jagged surface. Sometimes she giggled and grabbed at lights that flashed before her eyes, her eyes that glittered like the glittering eyes of birds that do not speak of these same things that we let go unsaid.

In those difficult months Yvonne Beauchemin tried to be the good neighbor, though her help was often inappropriate. The casseroles she brought to our house were overly spiced and made with leeks or fancy mushrooms, the kind of food my wife could not keep down. She also brought books that encouraged transcendental meditation as a therapeutic tool; when Yvonne left we cackled at her expense, my wife suggesting that her mantra be "Dilaudid." But in the early mornings, before the nurse came and I left for the office, when the surface of the bay would be glassy and scarved with mist, I'd often catch a glimpse of Yvonne in the round frame of my spotting scope, the blades of her paddle milling through the air like the legs of a complicated water insect. A shameless thought would enter my mind then, when I'd see her tracking sleekly across the water: a woman approximately my wife's age but vigorous in a way that my wife had never been, a woman who seemed to belong to a stronger and more perfect species. The shameless thought was that each of us had somehow chosen what we were, weak or strong, dependent or not. The foolishness of my theory became apparent to me five years later, when Yvonne Beauchemin became a bald woman just as my wife had been. And soon they'd become more similar still.

∾

SHE WENT THROUGH the trouble to print invitations to her party; perhaps this should have tipped us off. We her neighbors assumed that her being European somehow explained the odd formality, the sense of ritual—perhaps in her native Switzerland this was simply how things were done. We were intrigued, and we were flattered, enough so that all of us who were invited showed: the Carpenters and the Ritters and the Boldukes and the Schwartzes, four couples who remained intact, and the seven widows of Infinite Vistas who were not spending the winter in Arizona or cruising the Panama Canal. Plus me, the quirk, the man whose wife had predeceased him. Since her death, I hadn't fostered much of a social life for myself because it made me nervous, the way the women fluttered around me and spoke with the intonations of children. For years I'd set my stethoscope against many of their breasts, and I found myself also having difficulty switching tracks between their bodies and their persons. Bodies were easy: you thought in terms of what worked and what did not. But such analysis made for rocky conversation.

You can see why Yvonne Beauchemin's direct gaze, her no-nonsense manner, came as a relief. That she understood me was made evident when I arrived early at her party and she assigned me a duty that gave me something to do besides make small talk. My job was to take the coats from the women and pile them on the bed. One after another the linings slid from lightly perfumed shoulders with a crackle of electricity as the coats slumped back against my chest; underneath the women wore dresses or blouses that were slinky and bright. I noticed how most of them started drinking timidly, with sweet white German wine, but as the evening wore on they switched to red, an expensive Bordeaux that threw ellipses of ruby light across their faces.

Catering was done by La Maison d'Herbe, a restaurant located in one of the Victorian houses west of town. There were vegetables *en croute*, an assortment of pâtés, a cheese fondue with baguettes to be ripped and dipped, a duck served with orange sauce whose meat fell off the bone. A spinach salad with shredded crab, oysters on the half shell topped with cream, tiny lamb chops so tender they could be cut with the side of a fork. All this was set out buffet-style on the dining table, which had been laid with the good linen and the silver, the house lit up with many candles, each set in a crystal stick positioned among the masks and textiles that Yvonne collected on her travels. She stationed herself by the table, a position from which she presided over the army of teenagers who filled the plates and refreshed our drinks. Her black dress draped her body like a dancer's, her head covered in a smart, jet-beaded cap. I couldn't help thinking that this is one of the ironies of cancer, how it gives women the body they've always wanted as a kind of last bequest—the high cheekbones and flattened bellies. With us she exchanged pleasantries while simultaneously directing the teenagers with meaningful glances and tilts of her head. But I could tell that her attention lay elsewhere, as if she'd packaged it before the evening fell and already sent it drifting on her kayak.

Still, when I returned to the table for seconds she took my plate and began filling it herself, poking through the stuffed mushrooms with a disdainful look and moving on to the chops. "And how are your birds, Henry? Do you find the company of people as interesting as theirs? I must confess that often I do not."

I said that while the company may not be as good, the food is better. Then she blew a funny puff from her lips as she handed me my plate.

"Do you know what it means," she asked, "La Maison d'Herbe?"

"I assume you're going to tell me."

"House of Grass. A stupid name for a restaurant."

"Whatever it means, the food is wonderful."

She puffed again, and this time I recognized it as a derisive laugh. "You all are such provincial people. My dear Dr. Henry, if you'd ever been to Paris you'd know that this food is shit."

"La Maison de Merde," she said then, and laughed and laughed.

∾

JESSYE NORMAN was playing when we entered, the spire of her voice like a needle working heavy cloth, but somehow by the end of the meal Yvonne had segued to Chet Baker without our noticing. Dessert was chocolate truffles, a buttery pear tart, and a hazelnut torte, followed by cheeses and fresh fruit and cordials that we sipped from hand-blown vials. By this time the women were flushed and giggling like girls, and they began to touch me on the chest and shoulder as we spoke. Three of the men went into another room to watch the football playoffs, which left Dan Bolduke and me in the living room, whose heavy furniture seemed to clear a space around us as we stood there lapping at our syrupy cordials, a phenomenon that made me think I was truly drunk until I realized that Yvonne Beauchemin was going around and surreptitiously moving the davenport and chairs out of the way. Her breath shortened with each heave, causing her to stop and lean against whatever she was pushing, as if she happened to be seized by a sudden fit of reverie in the wake of the movement of each piece. Chet Baker was singing the standards I remembered from nights out with my wife back in the fifties, before we had children: "Time After Time" and "I Fall in Love Too Easily," even the idiotic "Look for the Silver Lining" ("and try to find the sunny side of life"). His notes, wildly shy of pitch, sounded as if they were coming through a heavy fog, his trumpet weaving through them like a line of birds in flight, filling the space between his verses. A voice, I thought, full of great reluctance to be here in this world. And the intonations were languid, as if he had resisted uttering the words until the last possible second, as if he had sent them here to this living room only when he finally realized that there was no other world for them to go to.

Then the women—how did this happen?—lifted their arms and began to swirl, swaying and bending from the waist. Dan Bolduke shambled around for a while like a good-natured oaf before he took up his wife and kissed her on the lips. When one by one the other women passed through my arms, I knew the feel of most of them, the moistness and density of their flesh. My patients, my neighbors: I am too old a man to have women for friends. And I thought it was sad that there were not more men for them to dance with, that they had no choice but to dance with each other, the way they did when they were schoolgirls.

And so it went through two dozen songs, an hour or more, until finally I boxed myself in a corner with Yvonne, whom I did not twirl under my arm but held firm against my chest in a proper two-step. Something Gershwin, maybe "Long Ago and Far Away"— just before the final chorus I took our outstretched hands and squeezed and pressed hers to my lips. I suppose the liquor made me giddy; I remember whispering a brief ode into her knuckles. "You are lovely inside" is the part I remember. So exceedingly stupid. At that moment I was just a child.

But Yvonne laughed and shook her hand from my grip, before handing me off to Florence Pratt. "No, Henry," she said, "I am rotten inside"—but Florence, having come in in the middle, did not understand the joke. And as we moved across the room I could feel the cloud of her befuddlement making its own weather in between us, as Yvonne danced an outrageous tango with Dan Bolduke, who dipped her backbone into an impossible curl while she clawed the air with one of her high heels, the white of her leg slicing through a slit that ran the full length of her skirt.

∾

WELL, HOW THE STORY ENDS, you know, same ending more or less as everyone's story. My wife, Yvonne Beauchemin . . . in the end all we can do is add them to memory's legions. Of course, my wife's is a different story, though sometimes I wonder how much different. Inside the body we are all much the same, just as a bird without its pelt of variegated feathers becomes a lump of undistinguished meat. And though it has been years since I've done any surgery, I remember in medical school being shocked by the sameness underneath the peeled-back human skin. Yes, you can see the tumor and the place where the broken bone has knitted back together— all the flaws that give us each our individual stamp. But these things are just a fraction of the body, compared with the bulk of what we hold in common.

ASHES

When his father died, Tim would have flown back to Chicago for the funeral, except that his father had insisted that there be none. "Why give everyone the chance to stand around jawing about what a son of a bitch I was?" he grumbled long-distance during the last days of his illness. "When I die, just throw me in the goddamn hole."

But the hole was a problem, because Tim's mother was buried in her family's plot from which Tim's father had gotten himself banished forever, after some bad behavior at the luncheon for the bereaved. And his second wife had years ago purchased a grave site for herself next to her first husband. Now she told Tim she'd decided "just to roll with" the plot she already had. Truth be told, her marriage to Tim's father never really took like the first one did.

Best thing, she offered, would be for Sam to be shipped out West, let Tim decide where to take it from there.

These last words frightened Tim, who was not sure what "it" meant. For a few days he expected Sam to show up on his doorstep in a giant box with his toes poking out like a bunch of grapes.

So when the UPS man dropped off only a modest box full of packing peanuts, Tim was relieved; inside was a smaller cardboard box with a metal cap, marked HUMAN CREMAINS. Also enclosed were his father's dog tags, and a bottle of Crown Royal whiskey in its purple bag, which Sam had bought when Tim was born, to be opened at his wedding. *Maybe it's time to admit defeat*, his stepmother had scribbled on a scrap of paper.

Go on, add it up, Tim dared himself as he clawed through the peanuts: this twelve-year-old whiskey had sat for another forty-three years inside its bottle. Bringing the total to fifty-five, whiskey old enough to join the AARP.

∼

TIM HAD TROUBLE thinking of himself as middle-aged; his young adulthood—the years his high school friends had married miserably and bred—he'd spent tromping around the mountains of the Pacific Northwest, working on and off in the Giffort Pinchot National Forest. Those days in the Giff: where had they gone? And how could they have left him with such a big gut in their wake?

One of Tim's friends from the Forest Service had settled in the same town—and hurried over when the box came. "Tim's wedding whiskey," Ivan purred. "The pretty purple baby."

"I've got the something old, and you've got the something borrowed," Tim said as he pried the bottle from Ivan's hands.

"Count your blessings, man." Ivan settled into Tim's battered recliner, kicking out the footrest. "If this was your wedding, you'd have a lot more people trying to horn in on the juice."

Tim poured two tumblers a quarter full and knocked glasses with Ivan before he swallowed. The whiskey gave him a suntan from the inside out.

"Aaah," Ivan exhaled from the back of his throat. "I could easily drink a whole fifth of this myself."

A hockey game flickered on the TV with the sound turned down, while on the stereo Neil Young lit into another screeching guitar riff. Tim's idea had been that he and Ivan, at this point in life his oldest buddy, would drink the whiskey with a quiet, ceremonial intent while Tim chewed on a few choice anecdotes about his father. But all he could think of was Sam standing outside, blasting the hose at dogs he suspected of shitting in his yard, Sam throwing his slipper at the TV, Sam borrowing Tim's BB gun to shoot the mourning doves burbling outside the window. Then Ivan began to play some serious air guitar, his head thrown back, his mouth a crater with a crumbling rim. Watching him, Tim felt himself getting annoyed at the fact that Ivan had grown the exact same beard as him without asking his permission. A U-shaped goatee without the mustache, something to gain a little cred with the high school kids, down whose throats each year Tim crammed the Louisiana Purchase.

"What's wrong?" Ivan asked, sitting up.

Tim shook his head. "Nothing." The bottle was sitting in the kitchenette next to the morning's dishes, the neck sticking from the felt bag like a headless aborigine shrugging from her frumpy dress. "Nothing except that it wasn't supposed to be like this. It was supposed to be me and my dad wearing cummerbunds and sneaking swigs behind the church."

"Oh, I had a wedding once. Believe me, it was overrated,"

"It's not just the wedding. Forget the wedding." Tim took the glass that Ivan handed him, full up to the rim. "I should be drinking this to celebrate something momentous, an event worth remembering for the rest of my life. Not, you know—" He waved at the apartment, the TV: "This."

"Hey, what's wrong with this?" Ivan blustered, sucking the sloppage from his hand. "Who's to say that thirty years from now you're not going to think back on this afternoon and say, *Boy, one thing I will always remember is that afternoon when my old buddy Ivan and I sat around watching the Blackhawks whomp the living bejesus out of the Pittsburgh Penguins. And we drank this bottle of the greatest hooch I've ever tasted.*"

"Yeah, right," Tim said with a rueful laugh. "The Pittsburgh fucking Penguins."

"And you know what?" Tim continued as his rue gathered steam, "I'll never be able to go back and see the Blackhawks play in the old Chicago stadium. Because I've got no one in Chicago now. And because they tore it down to build a new stadium just so the yuppies would have someplace to get their cappuccino—"

"Women like cappuccino," Ivan interjected. "The new thing is, you're supposed to bring a woman to the game—"

"Where they don't even serve the hot dogs with tomato wedges lined on top."

This led to a patch of silence, after which Ivan suggested absently, "You could always buy some tomatoes and cut them up and carry them around in a baggie in your pocket." But he didn't seem to be thinking about hot dogs anymore: he had taken the small box down from the bookshelf.

"What's a cremain?"

"Sam. Sam's a cremain." The little men on TV were starting to make Tim dizzy with their spinning. "The old Chicago stadium is a cremain."

Ivan unscrewed the cap and stuck his ear by the hole. "I think I hear Sam's soul crying out for freedom."

"The only thing Sam's soul is crying out for is that whiskey," Tim said. "Sam went to his grave wondering if his son was a homo or just a selfish little prick."

Ivan carried Sam's ashes into the kitchenette, where he splashed some whiskey in the box and stirred the ashes to a paste. "I'll show you momentous, buddy boy," he said. "Right after we kill this bottle we're taking your old man to the Giff."

∾

AROUND THE TIME that Tim went back to school to get a teaching certificate in history, Ivan had angled with an opposite tack in regards to what he called "the straight world": he'd moved to a cabin near White Pass where he would read the *Tao Te Ching* and live off the grid. But before the first snowfall, Ivan shot himself with his crossbow while trying to take down an elk, and the arrow so mangled the architecture of his leg that he would walk forever with a limp. *Shit happens, happened, will happen*: on the surface at least, Ivan let this conjugation roll off him with a shrug. Now he spent his days at the public library, where he wielded a light wand at the circulation desk, the computer going *Blip! Blip! Blip!* He said what he liked about this environment was its preponderance of women.

". . . and they walk up to you holding their books like a shelf for their breasts. Presented to you on a tray like the heads of St. John the two-headed Baptist."

This Ivan was saying as they hummed along the I-5 in his pickup, Sam's ashes on the seat between them, the sky souping up and the evergreens crowding in. Ivan had bought another bottle of whiskey to prove he wasn't just a mooch, an inferior bottle that Tim wasn't sure was worth reaching into another man's crotch to dislodge. Ivan was talking about a girl he'd been helping at the library, a student at the community college who was trying to go premed.

"And get this, I'm showing her how to search *schizomycosis* on the computer and in the middle of it she looks at her watch and says, 'Oops, I'm late for work, I gotta fly,' and when I ask where she works she tells me she's a dancer. So I go, 'You mean like Martha Graham?' only she doesn't know who Martha Graham is since she's Vietnamese, see, so I stand on my toes and she laughs and shakes her head and then—get this—starts wiggling around pretending that she's going to undo her shirt."

The truth was that Ivan had not dated anybody since his divorce some years back. Come to think of it, Tim had not dated anyone since Ivan's divorce either, and this thought troubled him—that Ivan's life might be exerting some kind of astral tug on his own.

"So what's she like?"

"Who?"

"The shickomytosis girl."

Ivan thought about it for a moment, driving along with his eyes closed. "Dang Kim Nhung is her name. She wants me to come see her dance."

"Don't do it," Tim said. "Remember what happened the last time."

"This is different—she invited me."

"Yeah, sure, they always invite you; they want to prove they're not ashamed. But how could anyone not be ashamed about having to hump a pole?"

Having said this, though, Tim wondered if he was underestimating women's shame threshold. At the few strip clubs he'd been in, the women looked terrifyingly smug, like his stepmother, if she were young again and wearing nothing but a cowboy hat.

To dispel the image, Tim tried wrestling the bottle away from where Ivan had it pinned against the wheel, causing the truck to zigzag down the road. Ivan would not let go until he took another swig and hollered out the window, "To the Giff!" Words that were swallowed by the whooshing, drooping, and not-quite-but-nearly night.

∽

SIX YEARS AGO, Sam had finally made it out to visit Tim in Washington, taking the Amtrak from Chicago. He got to town on a Monday and Tim had worked at school all week; his father passed the time by going for walks around the neighborhood. "Well, I don't get it," Sam concluded. "I thought there were supposed to be all these great big goddamn trees. If all's I wanted to see was a bunch of candyass little bushes, I could of just as well stayed home."

When the weekend came, Tim had taken his father out to the forest, and Ivan came too, as a sort of color commentator while Tim called the play-by-play: That's a silver fir, that's an alder, bigleaf maple, western red cedar. But Sam remained unimpressed. The spring day that was fair in town had been, in the mountains, cold and wet. Sam drank coffee from a cardboard cup and glared out the windshield. "So there's trees," he conceded. "But I don't see one big enough to drive through yet."

Tim planned to stop at a trailhead to show his father some of their old handiwork. He and Ivan had been on the trail crew, which besides clearing windfall mostly meant laying water bars: quarter rounds of cedar that channeled runoff from the trail. There was an art to wedging the logs so tightly that even a horse couldn't kick them out, and Tim wanted to see if their bars from a dozen years ago were still in place. In this one spot he was thinking of, Sam would have to walk just a hundred yards from the parking lot. Ivan had worn a long black oilskin cloak under which his bad leg swung as he leaned on his cane—after his accident, he'd exchanged his mountain gear for the wardrobe of an Australian vampire.

When they reached the trailhead, Tim could have broken out in tears: the bars had held, at least these bars looked old enough to be the ones that he and Ivan had set—he even talked himself into a déjà vu about their individual knots and nicks. A tricky spot, where the trail plunged downhill. Over the years the logs had risen from the ground, and soon they'd have to be replaced so hikers wouldn't stumble. And then the woods would bear no trace of him at all.

Sam contemplated the trail for a minute before his gaze swung back to Tim: "All those years, this is what you boys did?"

When they nodded, Sam shook his head. "Seems like a shame, to leave a perfectly good piece of fence post rotting in the ground like that."

∾

TIM MUST HAVE dozed off; when he woke the truck wasn't moving and the sleeves of his jean jacket were being strafed by colored light. Ivan had pulled off at the Skookum Club, a blinking nest of wires thirty miles east, in the foothills. Its sign stood on a tall metal stalk: a neon fir tree with breasts.

"Ivan, no," Tim groaned. "Let's not subject ourselves to

this again." They'd stopped here maybe a half dozen times before, once for each friend who got married, which in the course of things meant fewer visits as the years passed. Last time, as they were leaving, Ivan stopped to help one of the girls jump-start her car, and they'd driven off as she watched her engine box go up in flames.

"We'll just stay a minute, honest," Ivan assured him. "Let Sam catch a little pooty before we set him free."

No time to say that Sam had caught enough pooty back in the days when he could better appreciate it, because already Ivan was out and staggering toward the door. In his haste he'd kicked the bottle out of the truck and sent it rolling toward the dumpster. But Ivan didn't notice, focused as he was on the club's front door, where the bouncer made him open the box.

"Looks like mud, stinks like whiskey," the bouncer was saying when Tim caught up. "Okay, I'm stumped."

The bouncer was about to dip his fingers into the box for a taste when his flashlight struck the label, which caused his hand to snap back as if it had been burnt.

"What kind of kink is this?" he asked.

It was Ivan who looked down at his rubber sneaker tips before he answered:

"Grief."

∾

INSIDE, THE BASS NOTES throbbed at a frequency that interfered with the swallowing mechanism in Tim's throat.

First thing, he looked at the flimsy stage to see if the woman dancing was indeed wearing a cowboy hat. No, he saw with some relief, but she *was* wearing cowboy boots, white cowboy boots that she seemed afraid of stamping down too hard lest the entire stage collapse. Everyone looked as if they were packed in heavy syrup: a few girls traipsed around in their underwear, their trays bearing cups of coffee and glasses of soda pop. When Ivan finally recognized the girl from the library, planted like a lily in a forest of stumps, he shot up his hand and hailed her: "Dang Kim Nhung!" But her only response was to curl her lip and turn her back.

Tim saw that her buttocks were flat like a boy's, separated into their precincts by a purple satin ribbon. When he realized that she was dancing for two lummoxes who had been in his class a few years back, he tried to press himself flat against the darkness like a shadow. Still one of them cried out: "Yo Mister Fitz!"

The walls echoed: *Mister Fitz Yo Mister Fitz Yo Mister Fitz . . .* Or could have been a dozen of his students.

What she did was barely a ripple, waves traveling up her arms and then back down. Meanwhile, methodically, she touched various parts of her body, but not the parts he expected: instead her hip, her shoulder, an elbow, her knee. As far as Tim could tell, her legs were necessary only to hold up her torso within viewing range.

When the song was over, she approached them testily, grinding her gum between her teeth. "Library Man," she said, adding in a voice that would have been underneath her breath except that she was shouting to be heard above the din, "You have to call me Tiffany. What are you doing?"

"We were in the neighborhood," Ivan shouted back. "I was telling my friend about you."

She gave a shrug in Tim's direction before setting one hand on her hip. "Can't talk now; I'm working. But I could get you guys a soda. You still have to pay five dollars for them, though. Each." So they ordered two Sprites and watched the stage, where the girl in the boots took two steps in each direction, then agitated her hips. Stomp stomp hips. Stomp stomp hips.

"We came to see you naked," Ivan blurted cheerfully, when Dang Kim Nhung Tiffany returned with their drinks. By mashing her small breasts up toward her throat, her purple bra was able to manufacture the facsimile of a cleavage. To keep from staring at it, Tim watched the stage where the girl was wrapping up. Stomp stomp hips one last time, and then she curtsied.

Dang Kim Tiffany shook her head. "They don't want to put too much Asian onstage: I just do tables. And sorry, Library Man, but I think dancing for you would do a number on my head."

There were no stairs for the girl onstage to get down, so she had to inch off the edge while wriggling her white boots in the air. They had fringe that reminded Tim of the undercarriage of a carpet sweeper. Meanwhile, Ivan yodeled happily, *But that's the beauty!*

"You wouldn't be dancing for us, it'd be for his dad."

She glanced around the room then, as if expecting to

find him abandoned in a corner with a portable oxygen tank, until Ivan shook the box to make the clod thump.

"He's just ashes, see? Nothing you have to worry about."

Dang Kim Tiffany did not believe it until he opened the box and let her look, and even then she would not dance until Ivan offered her the contents of his wallet: twenty-six dollars. Plus his change. The bills she stuffed into her bra with the coins wrapped inside them. "Okay, Library Man," she said. "Just to show you I'm not sentimental about the dead."

She took the box and set it on a chair, and when the next song rose up, her wavery-arm dancing began, and again she touched strange places on her body. Tim could see, in profile, the restless movement of her lips, could hear her reciting the names of the bones: tibia, fibula, femur. "Cat Scratch Fever" was the name of the song the random universe had delivered up, and Tim watched the box shimmy along with the rumble of the bass, as if there were something live inside it.

When the song ended, she turned and handed the box to Tim. "Anatomy test tomorrow," she explained.

"You must have taken one of those time-management courses."

"You be surprised how much work I get done here. And practical experience: the other girls always want me to palpate their breasts." This all she shouted through the megaphone of her hands: "That means I feel them up! Everybody here is always freaking out that they got lumps! They bought themselves boobs, and now those bought-boobs are leaking! The bigger the boob, the more poison oozing out!"

❧

A WATER BAR was an insignificant thing, Tim realized, but its worth was easily measured: you kicked it and right away you knew whether or not it would hold. Water bars may have been at the low end of technology's food chain, sure, but still they were responsible for nothing less than the shape of the landscape, for the sides of mountains staying up, for one's way becoming or not becoming impassable with mud.

He'd wanted his father to understand this, but Sam hadn't, or Tim hadn't tried hard enough to explain. He was hoping that explanations somehow wouldn't have been necessary, that Sam would look down at the water bar and suddenly understand: how Archimedes was wrong about the size of the lever you'd need to hold up the world, how even a two-foot length of cedar could, with the proper placement, perform this feat. And then Sam would have looked up and seen the mountains rumpling and rerumpling for mile after mile, and he would have understood why his son had left Chicago.

But instead, to get out of the rain they'd gone to a diner in Packwood, where all Tim could think about was how his young mean father was now old and mean and weak, and it was Ivan who'd finally perked up with an idea over dessert.

"I know! I know!" he said as he tucked into his second slice of pie. "We'll take your father to see the Patriarch." The Patriarch was a tree that could be found on old maps, named by the forest's first explorers, an ancient douglas fir located on an unmarked deer path that took off from behind the trailers where they'd lived. When their work for the day was done, they used to sit between the roots of the tree with their backs propped against its trunk, drinking beer while the raindrops rustled in the branches. Silently, they would pay homage to their muscles flecked with dander from the woods. They would press the cold cans against their bruises.

This was where they were headed now, with Dang Kim Tiffany wedged between them in the truck. Hers was a snap decision, she said, brought about by the catalyst of Sam: once she'd danced for him, she felt compelled to see the ceremony's end. And she'd never been to the mountains, despite having lived in the Northwest since she was six, her own father being afraid of them because he said they were the home of ghosts. The storms were ghosts wagging their beards at the children who'd forgotten them too soon. And the gullies were where they reached over the mountains and scratched with their long fingernails. Her voice reminded Tim of a little bell being rung by an impatient woman.

"Every weekend he made us dig for butter clams. That's the story of my life: clams and more clams." She and her mother built driftwood fires and cooked lunch right on the beach. Dang Kim Tiffany was wearing Ivan's cloak because the boss had taken her pack, which contained her clothes, hostage. "No leaving with customers," he barked from behind the bar where he dispensed the soda pop. "Plus you got three more hours until you're off."

He'd seized one shoulder strap of the pack while she

pulled on the other, and—after they'd stood for a while at a standoff—she let go and sent him crashing into the glasses stacked in plastic racks.

"Who needs it?" she said as she crossed the parking lot in her purple underwear, in her silver high-heeled sandals that were now heaped on the floor of the truck like a pile of chicken bones.

Ivan asked, "So do we still have to call you Tiffany?"

Her earrings jingled when she shook her head. "It doesn't matter, Library Man. When I finish med school everyone will have to call me Dr. Dang."

They made the rest of the trip in silence, passing the reservoirs that stretched so ominously black between the foothills and the Pacific Crest. Dang Kim Tiffany fell asleep and snored quietly while drooling onto Tim's jean jacket, which he was surprised to find had more of an erotic effect on him than her dancing; it had been a long time since he'd found himself on the receiving end of a female slump. She breathed through her mouth, which smelled like hay, her nostrils small, her hair perfumed by smoke. When they finally stopped, he could hardly bring himself to wake her. Groggily, she sat up and said, "This is not what I expected of the wilderness."

They'd pulled off at a roadside clearing littered with paper diapers balled up in the brush. Their trailer was gone, and the concrete pad that it had sat on was now cracked and spiked with thistles. The tall firs that ringed the camp had been logged off, their stumps overrun with blackberry vines.

But the trail was where they remembered it, angling

uphill from the back edge of the clearing. Ivan beat back the brambles with his cane, while Tim took the rear and shone a flashlight at their feet. Dang Kim Tiffany refused their elbows and instead waded through the dark as if she were crossing a river, going by feel, her bare feet seeking out the bare ground where the deer had trotted on their errands. Ivan's cloak made her look like a dark shrub with a tiny human head. Whenever she stepped on something sharp, she'd flinch but not permit herself to say a word.

This was the same trail they'd taken Sam up when he'd visited six years back, though now, with the trailers gone, the undergrowth had reclaimed it. With Sam, they'd hiked slowly, and now they hiked slower still, Ivan humming "Cat Scratch Fever" and dragging his bad leg while a nearly naked woman walked behind him. So there was beauty, Tim thought, and also decay, and the years were just a factory for changing one into the other.

But the Patriarch was something that did not change— at least not perceptibly, to Tim's relief. A good six feet in diameter, big enough that each side of the tree had a climate of its own. Mossy on the uphill side, with roots that sat atop the soil like hands, the other side bare, the roots disappearing in the duff. Six years ago, when he finally reached the base of it, his father had tipped his head back and emitted one long whistle.

"Well, son, you got me," he said. "When it comes to trees, I'd call this one right here chapter and verse." But then immediately he'd turned and started walking back.

"Okay, I seen it," he called over his shoulder. "Now I

guess we can head on home." And when Tim opened the box and shook it gently to let the ashes scatter, they did not. Instead, the wad of them thudded to the ground and rolled into some prickly underbrush.

"That's it?" she asked. "That's what you bozos call a decent burial?"

No way, José, over her dead bod: she said Tim would have to fish Sam out and break him into pieces small enough for the wind to carry. Maybe they'd have to dry the ash to make it light enough: she dispatched Ivan to gather firewood.

"No green sticks," she called as he shambled off. "Do you even know the difference, Library Man?"

Ivan's voice came from the other side of the night's black wall when he said, "You may not believe this, but we were rangers once." And though Tim knew his father's send-off was getting way too complicated for this time of night, he also knew he had no choice but to follow the woman's orders. The first step meant finding Sam, and to do that he had to get down on his knees.

THE WATER CYCLE

1. ICE

Don't ask Aurora where she has been. Seventeen nights in seventeen different states, seventeen transmitters on seventeen different mountains. Clear across the country, only she was going backward: Idaho, Iowa, Tennessee, Maine, where somebody recognized her from the TV. TV is how we know what we know about Aurora, like that they found her in a town called Bath. Aurora living and not a dead girl. Seventeen nights, seventeen motels, seventeen Bibles in the nightstand. Seventeen buckets from the ice machine. It must have seemed like a vacation, no school and after all he *was* her father, though we did not know this when he stepped into Mr. Lentini's class, so quiet that we barely noticed him. We were doing the water cycle, Mr. Lentini showing three of us who did not know the trick how to make a cloud look like it had three dimensions. You had to draw some curves in the middle, not in an organized pattern, which looks fake.

And Mr. Lentini asked, *May I help you?* very polite before it clicked a second later about the shiny thing at the end of the man's arm being a gun. Then Mr. Lentini, who normally did not touch us though sometimes the girls wished that he would, scooping us under his arms, where there was a powdery b.o. smell. And saying, *Everyone under the desks*, soft enough that at first nobody moved until they saw Mr. Lentini pressing the three of us against him, which was how come everybody was jealous of us later on the most after Aurora. Who let the word *Dad!* escape from her like an animal breaking free from a trap. He had his arms in their camo-jacket sleeves wrapped all the way around her, the gun pointing out from the base of her neck. He was dancing her backward out the door, hugging her so tight the nubs of her breasts must have hurt, oh yeah he was touching her for sure but then again he was her father.

2. WATER FROM THE DITCH

Seventeen days in seventeen motels: meanwhile we were supposed to keep drawing clouds and rain and rivers as if nothing had changed, with arrows to connect them because Mr. Lentini said these were all versions of one thing. We put the mountains in the background, an arrow to show the snow melting down, another to show the vapor rising. Wiggly lines for the arrows' shafts. What the parents did was tie yellow ribbons around the trees out front because of some old song, never mind how stupid it sounded, to think that some old song could save her. Also there was Jake Dumfrey, the nighttime security guard from the mall, who stood by the flagpole wearing his fake foot from Vietnam. When we collected water from the ditch by the road both he and Mr. Lentini walked there with us, Mr. Lentini up front and Jake Dumfrey hobbling behind even though the ditch was just a few yards away, a trickle buzzed by flies. But under the microscope you could see that the water was not so simple as it looked: in the smudge of it there were creatures like the cyclops and the paramecium, the machinery visible inside them, beating. All day long people in cars passed by the ditch and didn't know about the creatures. But they knew about Aurora from the TV, from the newspaper and posters tacked on all the telephone poles in town. And from the yellow ribbons that made the cars honk when they saw us out there. Like they thought our soccer team had just won the tournament.

3. CLOUDS, AGAIN

Really it was more than seventeen days, because her mother kept her home an extra week after they found her, which gave Mr. Lentini time to warn us about not asking her anything when she came back, *Poor Aurora's been through enough.* The only difference was that her black hair was cut in bangs, and we wondered whose idea this was, because what if it was his idea but she didn't like it and now there was no way to grow her bangs back? We were doing the water cycle all over again so that Aurora wouldn't think she'd missed it. *Don't do anything that would make Aurora feel uncomfortable*, Mr. Lentini told us, and so we let her use the blue crayons even though there were not enough to go around, so that she wouldn't have to draw uncomfortable rivers that were red or purple. You could use gray or black and still have normal clouds. Aurora's clouds had spikes on them, like a collar worn by an angry dog, but Mr. Lentini wouldn't tell her they were incorrect just *Very interesting*. And when we came to the part where Mr. Lentini had to explain how clouds and rivers were all the same thing, Aurora raised her hand and contradicted him: *They're not.* He said, *Of course, I meant in a manner of speaking*, but her face stayed closed in an angry fist until he backed off. *Okay, Aurora, technically you're right: it's all water but okay okay it's not the same.*

4. RAIN

How things change: at recess, no one says *you dumbfuck* anymore, because we are afraid Aurora'd hear, and it might *slay her*. Also we stopped playing any game that needs an *it*, because we can't decide should Aurora be the it or not be it, like which would be less uncomfortable? Also Mr. Lentini stops letting us watch the mouse go in with the Alaska Pipeline, who is the boa constrictor who never does anything now except sit under the warming lamp inside his tank. Mr. Lentini used to let us stand there cheering sometimes for the snake and sometimes for the mouse only now all you can see is sometimes a lump squirming in the middle of the Pipeline's body in the morning when you get there. And you have to sneak a look so that Aurora doesn't see. But the truth is that she sneaks looks too, *she wants to see the mouse suffering.* Just watch her: all morning she'll dream up a million reasons why she has to walk by the Alaska Pipeline's tank, she's the only kid who's allowed to pee as much as she likes. Then in the afternoon, when school gets out, her mother drives up to the door to get her. If it's raining Jake Dumfrey even holds an umbrella over her head while she gets into their Ford Escort, just like she was a movie star.

5. THE RIVERS

Purple river, red river, yellow river, blue river: what's the difference, only a *dumbfuck* would mistake these for something real. After we draw the rivers, it's the same water from the ditch, Aurora getting to walk beside Mr. Lentini, Aurora getting to dip the beaker in. Yeah yeah yeah. When the cars go by she'll look up and they can't help it: when they recognize her they almost always hit their brakes. She's the ghost girl, the one from the TV, they want to honk but then they stop themselves and the horns come out sounding like little gasps. Then Aurora always gets first dibs on the microscope, but who cares. It's the same paramecium, same cyclops. Same seventeen motels, big deal. In all the towns the McDonald's would of been the same.

6. ICE

New clothes new barrettes new Hello Kitty plastic purse. New way of looking older when she looked out from her bangs. New dance steps from MTV new way of putting your hands on your hips and jerking them forward like you were in the middle of a car crash. New stupid world new stupid us. She ruled our lives and was our ruin.

7. EVAPORATION

You could not stay here if you were Aurora; it would only be so long before everyone could not hold the *dumbfuck* back and that would start the other words and then you'd have to get away. Which is what happened: she used the summertime for her escape. Before the sunny weather came, she vanished—before we saw her in her bathing suit, before anyone even got the chance to ask her about the ice machine. Like whether he let her go get it, the cubes of ice I mean, did he let her walk outside past the other rooms and the parked cars with the little plastic bucket the color of skin lighter than hers? Also if he took her to the swimming pool, if their room had cable TV HBO a whirlpool bath or a coin box attached to the bed for the magic fingers. Once

I saw him on TV being led in shackles from the court-house. But you couldn't tell much just by looking at him, a bald man in an orange jumpsuit. Like I wondered how he did the checking-in, if he made her duck down in the car while he asked for a room in back, if he made her wait there and then sneak in after dark. Or did he take her into the office with him, saying, "I need a room for one night for my daughter and me," his hand on her shoulder like anyone's dad. He'd of bought her a dress, he'd of bought that new haircut. And would she go along with it, because what he said was true.

SAINT JUDE IN PERSIA

Forget trying to argue with my sister about context—*the bad words are always bad*, she has decreed. This time the context is: I caught my sleeve on the spoon standing up in the jar of molasses and sent it thumping to the floor.

"What bad words?" I ask, playing dumb.

"You know. Don't try to trick me."

Louisa has gotten most of her ideas from her special education teachers—put them in a blender with a little of the Home Shopping Network and some MTV and basically what you come up with is a version of Emily Post who knows all the top ten hits. But my sister is also a woman of action, and when she sees the black goo making a run for it, moving like an amoeba, she puts on a pair of oven mitts and uses them to swat the flow.

"Actually, those are very old words given to us by the Anglo-Saxons," I say as I get down beside her with a roll of paper towels. "Words invented especially for people to use when they're in trouble," I add, and here my sister stops to scratch her cheek with a gooey mitt.

"You're not in trouble," she reports from behind her thick glasses. "You were just making cookies."

~

THE REASON I WAS BACK living at my mother's was that I had just gotten out of rehab, and the cookies were an attempt to get a little of the domestic thing going again. They'd put me on "administrative leave" from my job at the boat shop, which let's just say is not the kind of work environment where a little substance abuse is going to damage anyone's reputation, so long as you keep it to your nose and keep your hands out of the till. At the boat shop, we can all recite the TV commercials that come on late at night: *If you don't get help from us, please, get help somewhere* or *Saint Jude's Hospital—your comfort close to home.* Then Rusty the wizard of the inboards will put into circulation his version of a Beatles circa-1970 scream: *Ju-ju-ju Judy Judy Ju-day!* And all the other boat guys will join in with their howls and yips. *Aaowh!*

It was during my brief incarceration in the Saint Jude's rehab unit that my father let his bombshell drop, about the woman he'd had on the side for years and about how the time had finally come to cut my mother loose. She said, "That was always his plan, wasn't it? To stick the rest of us out there on the gulag so he would be free to conduct himself like a tomcat?"

The gulag she was talking about was the place my parents bought when Louisa and I were kids: crooked farmhouse on ten acres forty miles from town, half pastureland and half swampy alder forest, sandwiched between a U-cut Christmas tree lot and a junkyard. "And didn't I walk straight into his trap, letting myself be kept barefoot and pregnant out there in the wilderness?"—this said to me against the background *plink-plink* of the Saint Jude's Ping-Pong table. I figured there was no use in pointing out to Mum that she had not been pregnant since Spiro Agnew was vice president.

My explanation had always been that my father put those miles between us and the pulp mill where he was an engineer because every day then gave him the chance to display his knack for expediting anything that could stand to move a little faster. Forty miles to work, no problem—the distance he compensated for by driving ninety, roaring down the dirt roads in his Lincoln. When he learned there was no municipal garbage collection out there in the sticks, my father's solution was to buy an old backhoe from the junkyard, a yellow hulk spotted with brown primer that reminded Louisa and me of a giraffe. Cheaper than paying for a private service, he said. Of course, the trash piled up, waiting for him to get around to burying it.

Louisa stumped him, though, because for her he could come up with no quick fix. I've seen him walk into what he thought was an empty room, only to find the two of us quietly playing there, making our naked Barbies do the splits. And Louisa he'd stare at without the least quiver of recognition, like she was some wild child who'd just stumbled in from the forest. Then he'd ask me a question to dislodge the particles in the room that had congealed around my sister, something like, "Did you remember to brush out Mister Chester?"

Mister Chester was my father's horse, though he might as well have been a motorcycle or a magic carpet, since my father's main interest lay in the speed with which he could be conveyed. But Mister Chester was, at the end of the day, a horse, and that meant someone had to muck his stall and lance his boils and sop his pus, which was where I came in, the pus-sopper, boil-lancer, little miss mucker of the stall. This was why, though I am nowhere near the rider that my father is, Mister Chester had no choice but to tolerate me on his back. The horse was smart enough to realize that if he threw me and broke my neck, in no time he'd be living belly-deep in his own shit.

Shortly after the arrival of Mister Chester, Mum shamed my father into also buying a more docile creature for my sister, a pony the color of curdled milk, whom she named Mister Twinkie. I own only one photograph of her from the family's brief Mister Twinkie era: ten years old and cowgirl-hatted, her fists full of the pony's cotton-boll mane. She looks like she's found the place she was born to be, her and the pony giving off an aura of yellow light. You would not guess from this picture that Mister Twinkie would turn out to be just bad luck with four legs attached: mention his name now and all that light will drain from Louisa in the form of yolky tears.

What happened was that not too long into his time with us, the pony had a heart attack as it trotted along under Louisa's weight, and Louisa sank to the ground with three hundred and fifty pounds of dog food underneath her. Picture me as the littler sister watching from the far side of the field as the bigger sister squats bowlegged with the carcass in between her fancy boots. Even from a distance I knew that Mister Twinkie was dead and I knew that she did not, and I knew that my knowing forever changed the space between us. "Get up!" she hollered, and even tried to drag the pony a few feet, until I came across the pasture and explained that Mister Twinkie could not get up, he never would.

After this, it seemed my mother soured on the whole idea of country living. But at least the demise of Mister Twinkie gave the backhoe a chance to prove its worth. And while he was at it, my father dumped several weeks' garbage into the hole before he scooped the dirt back in.

∿

MAYBE YOU ALREADY KNOW that "desperate situations" are what Saint Jude is supposed to be the patron of, unlike other saints who could at least pull enough rank to get themselves saddled with a legitimate disease. Not Judas Iscariot with whom he is often confused, but Thaddaeus the apostle, brother of James. And what with his being decapitated by the Persians you might also imagine that he is not going to let anyone easily off the hook: after you get released from inpatient treatment, you're still looking at outpatient therapy for at least six weeks. Which means sitting around for three hours every morning with the other narcos, drinking coffee that tastes like it's been perked inside the hospital's incinerator with all the other medical waste.

How outpatient at Saint Jude's worked was that we went around the room delivering our bulletins from Loserville, the plots of which were all fundamentally the same: *I can't even make cookies without the whole thing turning into this great big goddamn fucking flop, so how the hell can anyone expect me to* dot dot dot, you can fill in the back end of the sentence with the hobbyhorse of your own ineptitude. The professional staff called it "sharing," one of the bad words in my book, but if you start quibbling about the nomenclature you can forget about them ever signing off on your paperwork.

Roger the therapist wears Birkenstock sandals that he slips off his feet to sit cross-legged in his chair, from which he reports in what is supposed to be a soothing yet forceful voice that we *are* good people and next time we *will* be able to make the cookies. Then he stands with his arms outstretched to give the author of this particular sob story a hug, only the majority of us are not huggers: instead we stare back at him through the steam rising from our coffee cups until Roger puts his arms down like a corkscrew folding up.

"Okay, you're not ready, I respect that," he says, and then it's on to the next person: *I can't even microwave a bowl of soup without the whole thing turning into a great big goddamn fucking* and on and on until you start feeling like you're stuck in one of those sci-fi time loops, and the three hours goes by like three thousand years.

You can see why it would have made me feel full of myself, to know that I could go home and spend my afternoons with Mister Chester, while the other narcos would be pulling second shift at the Tool-and-Die and biting their nails down to the quick. A little animal-human interaction, a few weeks of my mother's cream cheese and chutney sandwiches, and I figured I'd be back to my old life selling boats. I had the personal affirmations that Roger made each of us write for ourselves hanging in the kitchen—*LIFE DOES NOT REQUIRE YOUR PARTICIPATION* and *BEING A CURMUDGEON IS NO SIN*—those were the only two I'd been able to come up with that didn't strike me as the verbal equivalent of a yellow smiley face.

"What's a cur-mud-gee-on?" Louisa asked, squinting at the refrigerator door. I told her it meant a person who didn't want to be nice all the time.

"Everyone wants to be nice."

"I don't."

Louisa shrugged: "Maybe you'd be happy if you were nice."

"Who says I want to be happy?"—but of course my sister says I should be happy because I'm living back home with her and Mum, all of us gals together again at last.

"Plus we've got cable," Louisa pointed out, her voice warbling with glee.

∾

BUT THE IDEA that I had, through oversimplification, misunderstood the situation out there on the gulag (like: who *was* paying the mortgage anyway?) occurred to me one day when I saw my mother stepping out of the house with my father's Browning. She held the gun with both hands while she carried the box of cartridges by clenching the open box-flap between her teeth. When I asked what she was doing, she grunted, "Mmhm mhmm mmmh," until I took the bullets from her mouth.

"I want you to show me how to load this," she said, and then of course I'm dumb enough to ask her why.

"I want you to show me how to load this so I can fire it," she snapped. "Really. Must we proceed with these inane questions?"

My mother may be short and squat, a victim of too many shortbreads with her tea, but she's still not a woman you want to go up against when she's got a bee in her bonnet and a gun in her hands. So I drew back the bolt and showed her how the bullets fed into the barrel. Then I tried to show her how to brace the butt against her shoulder but at this point my mother strong-armed me away.

"I've got it. All right. Enough!"

She marched across the field to one of Mister Chester's jumps, a couple of logs that I had stacked. Along the way, she collected some Snapple jars from the piles of trash, jars that she lined up on the top log of the jump. She was wearing her rubber barn boots and a pleated skirt that stuck out from underneath her raincoat. When she raised the Browning I could see the ripples where her pantyhose sagged on the backs of her knees.

Boom! Her first shot knocked her over, and she went down like a tree, her knees locked so that when she landed, still clutching the rifle, the barrel pointed straight up from a clump of poppies.

"I won't have you mocking me," she yelled from that nest of orange flowers, from which she wouldn't rise until Mister Chester and I had ridden off. "Be gone, the both of you! Both you and that wretched hack."

Being the kind of animal who thrived on chaos in its sonic form, Mister Chester never flinched no matter how the branches rattled from her shots. And somehow it was thrilling, if you want to know the truth—to be the last remnant of a dying outpost while the enemy encroaches on all sides. In no time I started feeling like a member of the Polish cavalry riding toward the German tanks, the little cones raining down from the hemlocks to be crunched by Mister Chester's feet. With my recent attentions, his nut-brown coat had once again begun to shine the way it did when we were both kids, and when he galloped across the pasture he lifted his legs like a showgirl, like the sky was a camera and the sun was its bulb, flashing whenever a cloud sailed past.

And by the time we got back, I had to hand it to my mother: more often than not, she was hitting her marks. If the jar didn't shatter, she'd cry, "Bloody hell!" then fire again. I could hear her muttering like a chipmunk as I put up Mister Chester in the barn. Every time a bottle bit the dust, she went: "Hah!"

Inside the house, lost in MTV-land, Louisa was watching a guy prance around in a black leather contraption that exposed his buttocks whenever he turned his back to us.

"Bad manners," she said, wagging a finger at the screen.

"I think bad manners is the point."

Though the guy's bare ass was working its magic, still Louisa couldn't keep her attention from eventually turning to the outside world.

"What's Mummy doing? It's time for *Oprah*," she said as she peered out the living room's picture window, twisting herself into the drapes. When she turned around again, the video had changed to a troop of large-breasted women, very energetically dancing.

"What happened to the guy with the butt?" she asked suspiciously—like I had somehow deliberately made him vanish.

❧

IT TOOK ME a few days to figure out what she was up to, my mother, when I started coming home from mornings with the narcos and the two of them were gone. Well after sunset they got in, with half-ravaged cartons of take-out food and Louisa giddy, I could tell, from the adrenaline rush of some new unfamiliar form of guilt. My mother wore the collar of her raincoat turned up like a spy, and she even had on—I swear—dark glasses. Except that these glasses had rhinestones at the hinge.

When I asked where the two of them had been, Mum reported from somewhere high up in her sinuses that she was under the impression that one of the benefits of getting old was that you did not have to give a continuous accounting of your whereabouts.

"At least that's how it was explained to me by your father," she added, though this cynicism sailed right over Louisa's head.

"We got Chinese food," my sister said, holding up the crinkly sacks. "It's your favorite: pig and duck."

That night, in the car trunk, swaddled in an old pink blanket, I found the Browning and swapped it for an alder limb of about the same configuration. I could picture my mother cruising by the pulp mill until her path intersects my father's just as he gets off from work. Then Mum leaps out of the car, muttering something about being stuck out on the gulag with an addled child and a junkie, before she discovers that the Browning is now a stick and damns me to hell forever.

And this is part of what happens, or at least the middle act of it—the drama commences when my mother stops at a traffic light and realizes that she's pulled up alongside who else but my father: right-hand lane, wearing his tweed porkpie hat, *Carmen* blasting so loud that she can see his windows flex. There's too much traffic for her to stop and pop the trunk right then and there, so instead when the light turns green what she does is pull in behind him. And she rams him a couple of times, then tries to cut to his left to force him off the road, the only problem with this plan she's making up as she goes being that her car's a Hyundai while my father's in his Lincoln. With a little evasive maneuvering he could leave her in the dust, but instead what he does is give her what she wants, in this case meaning that he does pull off, he even gets out of the car in his stupid hat like he's offering himself to whatever punishment she wants to inflict. And my mother apparently takes some hope in that, that his willingness to let her kill him is his way of atoning for his sins, her gunshot his penance, his penance her forgiveness (& suddenly her plan changes—she will only graze him with a flesh wound), when in fact my father has stopped here only because he's noticed something that my mother in her homicidal trance has not, which is that the parking lot belongs to a substation for the state police.

But in the narrow focus of her rage, the percentage of cars in the parking lot that are cruisers does not click, as Mum grabs what she thinks is the gun from her trunk and shakes the blanket and the limb comes rolling out. In the meantime my father has stepped into the substation and is now striding her way with three troopers in tow, among whom my mother is suddenly whirling like a ninja, swinging at my father's head like it was a piñata full of shit, jabbing the limb like a bayonet every time she gets an open shot. She's shrieking all the Anglo-Saxon that she knows, carrying on like a Pentecostal jabbering in tongues, sunglasses slantwise on her face so that one eye shows Picasso-like above and one below, both of them bugged from the pressure of all the steam inside her head, the cause of which is curiously not my father but the woman who sits in his Lincoln with the windows rolled and all the doors locked— the terrified counterpart to terrified Louisa, who similarly cowers in my mother's car with her eyes shut and both hands over her ears.

Or at least this is my version, cobbled together from everyone else's, starting with the troopers' report. From the back seat of the Hyundai (this was after I called a cab out to the gulag so that, after throwing their bail, I could drive the felons home) my mother was not shy about painting me her own picture of events, the focal point of which being how she'd be damned if she was going to stand by and let her home be snatched from underneath her.

"You've always hated that place," I said.

"Well, I take comfort in surroundings for which I feel a touch of loathing," she snapped. "That's the British in me. Why do you think England has so bloody many chip shops?"

For his part, my father weighed in later that evening via the telephone, his version coming down to the bottom line that I could count on his pressing charges. "Your mother's not exempt from the rule of law," he said, "just because she's got a broken heart." All I've got to say to him is that he shouldn't flatter himself about my mother's heart.

And maybe it was Louisa's account that was the most unbiased, Louisa who was plied with quarters and taken downstairs to the vending machines. A lady policeman showed her how the handcuffs worked. "Then I was locked in jail with Mummy," she said, her terror having given way to exhilaration over her ordeal.

We were back in the kitchen, eating from a Styrofoam container of moo goo gai pan that I found in the glove box, my mother having retreated upstairs. Louisa's voice takes on a conspiratorial tone when she tells me, "Mummy got locked up for a bad word."

Which? I ask, but here my sister clams up.

"Come on," I say. "Was it the *F*?"

A sideways shake from Louisa's head.

"*S-h?* A-hole?" and now she starts giggling.

"Was it, you know, something British? Did she call the cops wankers?"

Louisa's dying, fit to burst.

"Dildo, dickhead? Douchebag? Dork?"

"No—it was the *C*!" she squeals, the baddest of the bad words because it is the female one. And this recounting of my mother's naughtiness has made my sister drunk with remembering her minor part in it. She can hardly contain herself when she reports, "That's what Mum called the lady."

"Which lady?"

"The one sitting in his car. The one who Mummy says has ruined everything!"

∽

THAT'S HOW OUR TIME on the gulag came to an end, because property values had gone haywire and we knew he would go after whatever he could get. My mother would end up she knew not where yet with Louisa, and I would get another moldy duplex for myself in town, whose other half would be occupied by a pair of teenage newlyweds, whose common wall would thump whenever he tied one on and sent her reeling against it. Of course, I was only projecting at this point, extrapolating from the data of the past, which I wasn't supposed to do now that I'd been rehabbed. Roger said that I should see my life as a ball of clay that could be molded into anything.

"But say I left the clay in my purse in the car, and say with the windows rolled up the whole thing got sort of baked and cracked so that when I go to take the clay out of my purse it crumbles?" Somehow we'd wound up back at the clay metaphor for about the thousandth time, and when I mention this scenario all the other narcos go: "Yeah! Yeah! What about when that happens?"

Roger rolls his eyes before letting them wander back to me.

"Well," he says, "an addict can make up all manner of excuses."

"You're saying there's no such thing as an accident?"

"All I'm saying is that adults take responsibility for their actions."

He's tapping his clipboard with his pen like he wants to move on, but I won't let him. "But Roger," I say, "think about it. All I've got are some dry clay crumbs. What the hell am I supposed to do with that?" He's giving me his thin smile, a signal that he's about to go into his default mode, which is whimsy.

"Maybe you have to use your imagination," he says.

"Like how?"

"That's up to you," he says without uncurling his lips. "Perhaps you could use the crumbs to make an hourglass."

∽

OKAY: JUST TRY telling this to someone like my mother— her life is clay, she can be anything, when the clay dries up she's supposed to put the crumbs inside an hourglass— when in fact her doofus of a public defender has already convinced her that she can be only one thing and that is Crazy, especially if she doesn't want to pull some serious time in the big house. He also told her that, since Louisa would likely be deemed an unreliable witness, I was the one who ought to carry the flag on her behalf. I guess I should have been flattered, since *reliable* is not a word that's been applied to me much of late, maybe not since the old days when I was my father's stable girl. Whenever the question was, "Did you remember to brush out Mister Chester?" I was perfectly consistent, I could always answer yes.

But to my surprise he did not appear; instead it was just me and Louisa and Mum and her lawyer, who wore desert boots and a plaid short-sleeved shirt with one of those lumpy wool ties squared off at the tip. They held the competency hearing in the modular building outside city hall, in a drop-ceilinged room completely lined with mustard-colored indoor-outdoor carpet, which was where I got up and told the judge about how my mother'd taken to leaving food in the glove box, about how she stood there muttering to herself when she first shot the gun, and to make it a stronger scrap for the story I had her babbling a mix of William Blake and Edgar Cayce. Plus I put her in her nightgown when she lies down in the poppies and will not get up. After all, how much difference is there between a nightgown and a raincoat? I mean, is God really keeping that close a tab on the nomenclature himself?

So it was a victory, of sorts, when the judge ruled that my mother would just spend two weeks in the loony bin— at the end of which time he'd leave it to the doctors' recommendations. "Piece of cake," I told her. "You'll get out with more pot holders than you'll know what to do with." The psych ward at Saint Jude's is in a different building from the rehab unit, but sometimes our nurses would stop by the psych ward to borrow supplies for arts and crafts. They were afraid to let the populations mix for fear the narcos would start hitting up the psychos for their meds.

All this I'm explaining in my mother's bedroom as she packs her pink suitcase from the sixties with the plastic wood-grain trim. She wanted me to advise her about what she should wear to be a crackpot, and I said that was the beauty of being one: at last, you get to wear whatever you want.

Late that afternoon my mother comes downstairs with the suitcase, the shoes she's selected pinched between the fingers of her free hand. They're her good heels—she must have decided to go Classy Crackpot—and I can tell that she's making a performance of her leaving, which is, after all, just a rehearsal for the more permanent leaving that will come later, when my father cuts her loose without a cent. Already he's told me that after my mother leaves he'll send a trailer down for Mister Chester, whom he plans to board at a stable near his new house overlooking the Puget Sound.

"I guess it's time for one last perambulation," my mother says, after setting both suitcase and shoes beside the door. Through the picture window, I watch her feet slide into her boots on the steps and walk toward the barn, which is in truth little more than a shed, a cockeyed structure whose rotting silvery frame contains just enough room for Mister Chester and the winter's stockpile of hay. My mother goes in and leaves the doors open, and soon Mister Chester comes walking out; when she comes out after him she's once again got the Browning in her grip. She must have found it where I had it stashed between the hay bales, and for a minute when she hoists the gun I think she means to kill. *Okay, I will let her have him*, is what I say then to myself, because in nobody's mind but my own was Mister Chester ever anything other than my father's horse. As my mother has pointed out, all those years I was gone, living in town, what good was I? *What good was I?*

But when the shot cracks out, instead of dropping, Mister Chester fixes my mother with a look that is clearly his horse-language way of telling her that she can go fuck off. When she fires again, Mister Chester picks up his pace only the merest notch as he saunters toward the woods. I realize then that my mother's got the rifle tipped toward the sky, that she's not trying to kill him but only drive him off. *Life does not require your participation. Being a curmudgeon is no sin.* Once Mister Chester blurs into the landscape's sepia-colored edge, she twirls and empties the rest of the bullets into the barn before throwing the gun into the dirt.

"What's Mum shooting now?" Louisa asks, without too much concern: Louisa's memory is like a wake that closes up behind her as soon as she moves on.

"Just the barn," I say to my sister, who doesn't look up because she's mesmerized and letting her body sway. She's watching MTV again, standing so close the jump cuts splash their colors into the white screen of her face.

"Why's Mummy want to kill the barn?"

The amazing thing is what happens next, when my mother stomps from the barn to the backhoe sitting some thirty yards off, parked among the burn barrels like the skeleton of something that had just been exhumed from the dirt, its yellow spots reduced to freckles, its tires caked with last year's mud. What's amazing is the magic she works to get the ignition to turn over, and the way that, after much fiddling with the shift, she somehow manages to bring the machine to life. Suddenly she's in gear, moving *chink chink chink* toward the barn from the far side of the pasture, her raincoat flaring from the ancient driver's seat while the bucket scrapes along the ground. It looks as if she's trying to build enough speed so that when she plows into the barn the whole thing will go down; she's angling toward one corner where the footings are especially cracked.

By now it's dusk, and dribbling out of the backhoe's seat are particles of foam rubber that look like snow as they're seized and carried by the wind, over and through the crowns of the naked alders. An A-1 sunset has just started to creep from cloud to cloud, and I have to yell above the music for my sister to come get a load of this, as our mother, furious and wild-haired and small, steadies herself behind the wheel.

ANYONE ELSE BUT ME

"Don't try to make anything burn" is Marco the instructor's first piece of advice to the class, which the YMCA catalogue had listed as "Skipping Through Life": somebody's idea of an upbeat name for the senior citizens' women's exercise group. Ruth's enrollment fee had been a gift from her daughter, who said, "Ma, you're turning into a lump." And indeed, Ruth is hard in the running for fattest person in the class, though, her daughter's opinions aside, she is not all that fat. It's just that the other women are surprisingly firm for a bunch of . . . well, old ladies.

Ruth also guesses that she's the youngest old lady here, fifty-six, barely squeaking over the wire that was the minimum age for the class. Marco himself looks some years younger, husky but toned, a city bus driver who leads the class during his lunch hour, he explains—"to keep the pizza out of my mouth." Soon Ruth realizes that these introductory comments are meant for her, the rest of the group having been through this routine on countless noons. Her outsider status is also made clear by her sweatpants, which no one else but Marco is wearing. The rest of the women are dressed in coordinated leotards.

"I won't be giving much instruction," he tells her as he warms up, lunging from side to side with his fists on his hips and his legs spread. "I think you'll be able to follow along. But if you have any questions, give a shout."

Then Marco punches a button on his tape deck, from which bursts the trumpet intro of an Andrews Sisters number, "Boogie Woogie Bugle Boy." Abruptly the women line up and begin to march in a circle, swinging their arms. As Ruth imitates their movements, she can't help thinking about the goose step she play-marched with, back when she was just a kid. And how did it happen that one day you're playing Hitler in the alley and before you know it you're in the senior citizens' women's exercise class, where the instructor's calling out, "Big steps, ladies! Big steps!"?

∿

PRAIRIE ROSE, her daughter, works for the town's Miracle Management Response Team, which has been made necessary by the appearance of the Virgin Mary in the dark stains running down the concrete seawall that can be seen from the bridge over the inlet that bisects town. Prairie Rose complains about how working for the MMRT is not all it's cracked up to be: mostly you just walk around in an orange vest, picking up trash. The viewers of the miracle gather on the bridge and in the marina parking lot, where concessionaires charge five dollars for a ride out to the base of the seawall to touch Her. In the parking lot the viewers leave behind not just rosaries and candles but also a surprising number of wadded hamburger wrappers. "I mean, personally, I think of Mary and I think salad," Prairie Rose says, "but the evidence suggests that she's got everyone else hankering for red meat."

Prairie Rose took the job with hopes of being transferred to the city grounds crew once the apparition fades. She has visions of herself kneeling in bark mulch, changing the flower bed that spells the city's name from tulips to marigolds as the seasons cycle through. In the interim, she says she's just biding her time—"until ol' Mary decides to beam herself back up."

Of course, Prairie Rose has explanations, some kind of chemical the concrete was treated with, but Ruth is not so ready to write the Virgin off. More than once, she'd found herself standing on the bridge whose stone balustrades were now globbed with candle wax. All around her, people muttered prayers and worried their rosaries, while below them a flotilla of boats vied for position, overloaded with spectators who made the small crafts lurch as arms strained toward the seawall.

Being part of so much humbled humanity, even Ruth felt her heart begin to stretch until the bag of it touched the underside of her skin, and the contact discharged something on the order of a static shock. It was all she could do to keep from crying out.

"Oh, Ma, you're like all the other nutballs," Prairie Rose

told her. "You believe it because you've got nothing else going on in your life." But Ruth had to fight her impulse to go to the bridge too often, because she worried that the miracle would be rendered meaningless through overexposure, as she concluded it had been for Prairie Rose.

∾

WHEN PRAIRIE ROSE was growing up, Ruth had lived with a Mr. Lindquist, a formal man whose formal name Ruth first started using as a joke, before it stuck. He was some years older than she, an Air Force pilot in WWII, and Ruth had thought it odd—and so did not allow herself to think about it too much—that a man of his generation would never have proposed to her a formal marriage. Perhaps this had to do with Prairie Rose, to whom Mr. Lindquist's advice was usually prefaced with, "Look, now, I know I'm not your father . . ."

During all the years of his not-quite-fatherhood, Mr. Lindquist had spent his early mornings tinkering with a light aircraft he was building in the garage, which was what killed him in the end. The search and rescue squad found him dangling from a tree limb, pieces of the fuselage dotting the evergreens like shiny ornaments.

What money he left Ruth was modest (the bulk of it went to his son, a stand-offish man not much younger than she was): enough to support a woman who does not drive and who shops the canned goods stacked in the supermarket's Wall of Value. Prairie Rose had already left home and embarked on a series of disastrous relationships with men she would in the end denounce as helpless. *Helpless!* In her segues between boyfriends, she often moved back into the walk-in closet off the living room in Ruth's apartment, where she slept on a futon mattress.

She was a strapping girl who could run for miles along the inlet without breaking a sweat, and she kept her weight bench on the sagging front porch of the old house whose upstairs Ruth occupied. Even when Prairie Rose was not living in the closet, sometimes Ruth would wake in the night to the loud clink of the barbell being set down in its keeper.

So when Prairie Rose said, *Ma, you're turning into a lump*, Ruth knew this was not just an appraisal of her body but also of her life, for the truth was that ever since Mr. Lindquist died—okay, since even before Mr. Lindquist died—she'd really never (as they say) "done much." She'd raised a daughter, for a while she'd worked part-time at the library shelving books: wasn't that enough? But the answer was no, at least not according to Prairie Rose. Just one class, just one hour each day, Prairie Rose doesn't understand how anyone can be overwhelmed by this.

Ruth tries to explain how first there are the preparations to attend, the purchase of exercise clothes and the daily packing of one's duffel bag, then the getting dressed, the breakfast, the bus ride, the transfer, the other bus ride, the class and the shower and the reversal of bus rides until finally the getting home and fixing lunch.

After this, she is tired enough to indulge herself in a little nap, then maybe in the afternoon she ventures out to the library or walks down to the inlet, before returning home to fix dinner for herself and (often) Prairie Rose, for whom she buys vegetables and assembles them into a meal whose creation and cleaning up will fill her evening. Prairie Rose doesn't understand how her mother could be satisfied with so little; Ruth doesn't understand how a person's life could accommodate much more.

And then there is not just the exercising itself but also the mandatory socializing that comes with it. When they lie down for leg lifts, the women clump in groups to rehash the events of the twenty-four hours since they last lay down together. They know the routine so well they have no need to look at Marco or hear what he's saying, nothing to impede the speed and fluency of their chatter. And Ruth panicked when she first realized that signing on with the exercise group obligated her to participate: at first the women were satisfied simply to instruct her in technique, winching up her leg like a dog's for the exercise that Marco called "The Fire Hydrant."

But when the women turned onto their backs for pelvic tilts, a headband-wearer in a nearby clump called out, "So what's your story, hon? You a widow?" Ruth wiggled her head in a manner that she hoped could be read as either yes or no.

"Kids?" the woman persisted, but this time Ruth could not even muster the hint of a shrug as she lay flat on her back.

Then she heard the woman whisper to the pelvic-tilter next to her, "I think she's deaf."

Within the hour this rumor had worked its way from

clump to clump, and from then on the women no longer tried to speak to her but merely torqued her body into position whenever they were of the opinion that she was not correctly emulating Marco. Ruth didn't see the need to disabuse anyone about her deafness; she didn't want even one drop of whatever power was left in her creaky body to be dissipated by jawing. Being deaf streamlined her commerce with the other women to its bare essentials. Being the deaf woman set her free.

And when Ruth walked out of the Y that first day and boarded the bus for home, she was surprised to find Marco behind the wheel, wearing a blue city jacket and driver's cap in addition to his sweatpants. He seemed to avoid her gaze deliberately, which made her wonder if the code of conduct for exercise instructors was anything like that of therapists: you did not acknowledge your clients outside the session, giving them the courtesy of not giving them away. But later Marco caught her gaze in the rearview mirror, and when they stopped for a traffic light he took his hands from the wheel and began making peculiar gestures. This bewildered Ruth until she realized that Marco was speaking to her in sign language. In response to which she tried to nod inscrutably, as if she understood what was being said.

∾

WHEN PRAIRIE ROSE was a child, she took Mr. Lindquist in stride, but as she grew up that stride became a typically teenagerly sulk in pursuit of what Prairie Rose came to refer to as the Truth. Finally, Ruth made the mistake of admitting that, as far as Prairie Rose's biological father was concerned, there were several possibilities.

"So what you're telling me is you were easy," said Prairie Rose, *easy* being a word whose connotations in this regard she'd just picked up in high school. Ruth remembers exactly: they were sitting in Prairie Rose's bedroom, in the "regular" house they'd occupied when Mr. Lindquist was alive, the room's pretty lilac walls only a few months away from being repainted black and covered with posters of heavy metal bands.

"Well, I guess that's how your grandmother looked at it," Ruth said.

The upside of the "easy" remark was that it gave her an excuse to stalk self-righteously from the room, as if she had been wounded. And acting wounded saved her from having to explain—how when Prairie Rose was a baby Ruth had stared at her for hours and still not been able to reach a conclusive verdict. By the time Prairie Rose grew out of her baby flesh, Ruth could no longer remember much about the faces of the contenders.

"Look at me, Ma," Prairie Rose would say from time to time over the years. Then she'd hold Ruth's face between her palms while Ruth stared back while Prairie Rose squeezed, as if the information were in there somewhere and could be extracted like orange juice.

"Honey, I'm drawing a blank, I'm sorry," was all that Ruth could say. And Prairie Rose would squeeze her face for a moment longer, hard enough to hurt, hard enough to make sure it hurt, before she'd finally let her mother go.

∾

MORE RECENTLY, when Prairie Rose got on a jag and pestered her about the list of candidates, Ruth said there had been a meat cutter named Bill with a bubble of curly hair and a blond boy named Phil who lived with his mother off Delmar Boulevard in St. Louis, where Ruth had briefly attended nursing school in 1976. Or maybe she had the Phil and Bill mixed up, she wasn't sure anymore. During the month in question, she'd also traveled with her girlfriends to the Mardi Gras in New Orleans, where she had to admit there had been indiscretions.

"What do you mean, indiscretions?"

"Oh, honey, think about what you did when you were twenty."

Then Prairie Rose was quiet for a moment, as if she really were thinking. "So it's the butcher, the baker, or the candlestick-maker," she finally erupted peevishly. "Or maybe it's Dennis Hopper and Peter Fonda, who just happened to roar into town on their choppers!"

The problem was that Prairie Rose never wanted the kind of information Ruth remembered, particularly the car upholstery, in one case a maroon brocade deeply quilted with silver fixtures—door handle, ashtray, button for the electric window. This was where the boy, whoever he was, suddenly glided his hand under her bra, and in the midst of the squirming she usually did at this juncture, a new thought occurred to her: Why not?

It must have been twelve-string guitars that came into fashion that year and made those jangling sounds on the radio, sounds the boy used as an accompaniment when he performed his trick, like the *fwap-fwap* fluttering of a dozen doves pulled from a hat. Good God, what noises he was able to draw from her, and with only that one simple piece of equipment: his hand. It amazed her, doubly so when she learned about the portability of the trick, how it did not have to be *this* particular hand in *this* particular car, it didn't even have to be in a car at all but also could be made to happen under the live oaks in New Orleans, the moss spongy underneath her and no music there at all.

Now part of the reason Prairie Rose has to spend her days poking at trash left behind by the miracle's viewers is that she's recently entered into a contractual agreement with an outfit called BioFinders, and this costs big money. BioFinders guarantees that they will be able to locate Prairie Rose's father, no matter what slim pickings she's giving them to go on. The logo on their stationery reads, *The World Is Small for the Persistent.*

What comes first in the mail is a thick trifold of green xeroxed sheets, to be completed by Ruth in as much detail as she can remember. They want to know every incident she'd been a party to between January and April of 1976 "that either culminated in the discharge of semen *or* vaginal penetration without apparent ejaculative discharge." Start with January and work forward. Eight pages provided in all, with the instructions to use plain lined paper if additional sheets are needed.

"Must we do this?" Ruth asks, after skimming over the forms.

"Darn tootin'," is Prairie Rose's response. "Ma, you have no idea what it's like to go through life without a father."

"What was wrong with Mr. Lindquist?"

"Nothing!" Prairie Rose rolls her pupils back into her head and drops her eyelids over them. "This has nothing to do with Mr. Lindquist. This is about my life, Ma. The world doesn't revolve around your inadequacies."

Later, Ruth has to fight her way to sleep, against the clank and growl that is Prairie Rose bench-pressing more than her own weight.

∾

WHEN RUTH FOUND herself pregnant, instinct told her to run. She packed her things and headed west, and when she hit the ocean and could go no farther she tossed a coin and made a right-hand turn. So Prairie Rose grew up on Puget Sound, and happily it seemed, and Ruth was happy during her years with Mr. Lindquist, who drove a Chrysler and liked the big bands, not what he called "that caterwauling on the radio."

Of course, when he died she'd grieved, though her sadness was tempered by her not being sure whether he himself would have been sorry. He was getting old after all, and the Air Force body he had been so proud of was starting to fail, his prostate removed the year before. At least he'd been able to finish the plane before the cancer could make him weak, for Mr. Lindquist—who'd dropped bombs and been a POW—was not afraid of anything except maybe dying before he got the last piece into place.

Some people are like that, she thought: They need to get all the pieces into place. They want the precise orchestration of the big bands, not the jangling.

And it was remembering this that finally caused Ruth to spread out the green sheets and commence writing. Her entries varied from a few sentences to pages of her large script. All told, she remembered clearly just four boys from the months in question, though one's semen had only landed on the outside of her panties and she was not sure whether this should count.

∾

WHAT MARCO PLAYS at the exercise class is Mr. Lindquist's music, "Boogie Woogie Bugle Boy" and "Don't Sit Under the Apple Tree": the women march and skip while Ruth, the deaf woman, includes herself at neither the tail nor the head of the line but settles someplace in the middle, a position she deems least conspicuous. She no longer needs their postural corrections when they lie on the floor for pelvic tilts, nor do her muscles resist with such vehemence that she can think of nothing else. Instead while she exercises she can let her mind wander to Mr. Lindquist, and how she'd loved him in a way that was not jangly at all.

Sometimes after class instead of changing buses at the transfer station she stays on Marco's bus, his route taking her west to the bridge over the inlet and beyond that, the shopping mall. Sometimes she rides with him all the way to the mall but more often she gets off at the bridge to stand and gaze at Mary, whose features, Ruth realizes one day with dismay, are definitely, slowly fading. The folds of her wimple have all but disappeared and her toothy smile has lost its outer edges, becoming so blurry that it's hard to tell if her lips are turned up or held level or, indeed, whether the Mother of God is frowning.

But Ruth's concentration is broken when she also realizes that it's Prairie Rose on duty behind the seawall, wearing her reflective orange vest, megaphone in hand. She is telling the people jockeying in boats below to sit down and keep their life vests fastened. "Oh, yeah?" yells a man standing up in a Boston Whaler, "and what if we don't?" Prairie Rose bullhorns back that noncompliance is a maritime offense for which she's authorized to issue summonses.

"I think I heard that kind of talk before," hollers the man in the boat. "From a guy by the name of Pontius Pilate!"

∽

THE SUDDEN FADING of the miracle causes battle lines to be drawn among the citizens of town. There are those who believe the Miracle Management Response Team ought to be given the task of erecting a tarp to shade Mary's face from the sun, a sort of visor for which a frame would have to be built atop the seawall. This proposal is supported mostly by the shopkeepers, whose tills have been fattened by the constant flow of tourists. And then there are those who are sick of the town's being inundated by cars with I BRAKE FOR RAPTURE bumper stickers. Poison-pen letters start appearing in the local paper; the anti-miracle faction is accused of having a pro-homosexual agenda, the sunshade contingent of crass commercialism sailing under the flag of piety.

One good thing about the fading, at least according to Prairie Rose, is that it's caused the amount of litter to decline: "I guess they think it's Mary's way of telling them the party's over." But she herself has grown nervous about what will happen when the apparition disappears. She's heard a rumor that there are no openings on the grounds crew, that the odds are more likely she'll be laid off once the Virgin flies the coop. And this worries her, especially since she's just plonked down eight hundred dollars for a computer so that she didn't have to head down to the library every time she needed to communicate with the BioFinders.

So far what they've done is place personal ads in the newspapers of St. Louis and New Orleans, ads inquiring after anyone who knew one Ruth Horowitz in the mid-seventies, a blond-haired, blue-eyed, five-foot-six, 110-pound nursing student. They've also made inquiries via the meat cutters' union and posted notices on the "Mardi

Party" website, a chat group for people who attended the Mardi Gras in years past and want to reminisce. All of which Prairie Rose could have done herself, but BioFinders also guarantees that they will screen the crackpots and forward only those respondents who are Prairie Rose's IPBFs ("identified potential biological fathers").

Late at night, Ruth can hear the keys being tapped in the walk-in closet, where Prairie Rose sits on the futon with the computer planted between her legs. The idea of Prairie Rose telling the whole wide world about her mother's behavior, so long past, makes Ruth feel as though there are worms entering between her own legs and crawling up inside her. Worms that are not even real words or worms, but particles zapping through the air, zapping right in front of her nose as she tries to sleep while all night Prairie Rose's computer keys go tippy-tippy-tap.

With nights like these, the hour she spends each day skipping through life becomes her raft. Marco yells, "Big steps, ladies, shoot those knees up to the moon!" and they march around in circles, they sashay from side to side, they skip through an obstacle course of hula hoops. One Wednesday the headbanded woman skips so exuberantly that centrifugal force sends her crashing into a wall, which her head strikes with a hollow whomp that echoes off the cinder blocks. In its wake, the woman lies motionless, her mouth opening and closing like a fish.

Marco asks her, "Can you speak?" as the woman struggles to get something out.

"No," she says weakly.

The women gather around to help their classmate to her feet, Ruth among them and suddenly piping up, insisting that they not move her. And while they wait for the paramedics, Ruth holds traction on the woman's head, Mr. Lindquist having insisted that she always keep her first-aid card current. It was the duty of women who hitch their carts to older men, he said, just in case they ever needed CPR.

"Or the kiss of life," he said, poking her.

And now, bracing the woman's head between her palms, Ruth looks down at the face and is ashamed . . . because even after all these weeks she doesn't know the woman's name, she simply hasn't paid attention. *Angela*, the other women chant as they try to call their comrade back into the world, her lips testing and rejecting many of the common prefixes as if she cannot decide which word it would be worth her breath to speak. "Angela," Ruth repeats with them, holding the woman's head and stunned by the thought of what this skull in turn might hold, the whole contents of a woman's life.

"Angela, say something," she says.

∾

LATER, WHEN RUTH HEADS HOME on the bus, she's the only passenger except for one rumpled soul asleep on the back bench seat. Marco's talking at her across his shoulder: "Jeez, if I'd known you were a nun, I would of asked you sooner what you think." After Angela had sprung to her feet and, with a smack of her hands, announced that she was ready to get back to work, and after they'd insisted against her wishes that she ride off with the paramedics, the women had remained in a circle around Ruth and would not disperse until she came up with some plausible reason why she'd let them think that she was deaf.

"Oh . . ." she demurred, before seizing on the first explanation that came to mind, "for spiritual reasons I took a vow of silence." And from the way the women turned away from her in the locker room when she undressed, it dawned on her: they thought she was a nun.

"What I think about what?" Actually, Ruth finds herself relieved not to have to be the deaf woman anymore, having long ago worn out her repertoire of shrugs and gestures.

"You know, the Virgin—come on, I know you've looked. Looks like some kind of chemical oxidation to me, if you rub your fingers on the concrete they'll come up a little purple on the tips. But then I figure, what's the difference between oxidation and a miracle anyhow? It's like a rainbow—you could explain a rainbow using numbers. But when you look at it you don't think about numbers. The first thought that pops into your head is miracle." This last word Marco pipes through the trumpet of his fist, his pinky and ring finger wiggling.

"So what do you think?" he repeats.

"About the Virgin? I'm not sure what she is."

Marco cocks an eyebrow her way through the rearview. "I thought you nuns were in the business of being sure."

"Actually, I'm not a nun."

They are stopped at a light, and now Marco turns

around with his blue sleeve draped over the driver's seat. "Then what are you?" he asks.

Ruth shrugs, thinks about it.

Finally she says, "I guess I am only a skipper through life."

∾

THROUGH THEIR INQUIRIES with the meat cutters' union, BioFinders comes up with a man who matches one of Ruth's fragments, a man with whom Prairie Rose one day announces she has been corresponding.

"I think he's the one. He knows you, Ma."

"What does he know?"

"He knows the way you blink when there's something you don't want to talk about. The pretend-blink. The way you shut your eyes and leave them closed too long, like you're hoping the world will go away and leave you alone."

Like her, Prairie Rose says, he is broad-shouldered with brown eyes and auburn hair. Like her, he favors flannel shirts and boots. Like her, like Prairie Rose Horowitz, who has made Ruth crawl into the closet to witness something, the computer gleaming like an eyeball in between them.

"Can't you shut that thing off?" she says. "I thought you wanted to talk."

"No, I wanted you to come in here and see this."

"Oh, honey, I don't know if this is such a good idea. I read about men shanghaiing girls all the time using these computers. Before you know it you'll end up God-knows-where in some motel."

In the cramped space, Ruth tries to pivot around so she can crawl back out of the closet. But Prairie Rose says, "Wait a minute, this is why I called you in here. He's sending us a picture. He's gonna prove who he is before he makes you say who you are."

Ruth is on her hands and knees, and now she crab-walks sideways back in the direction of the screen, which ticks and hums as dots assemble at the top of it. Then the dots become lines, and the lines thicken into an oblong: the brow, the white of the eyes, the head angling one ear their way. Some strange bright speck contorts its shape.

"What's that?" Ruth asks.

Prairie Rose inches toward the screen and squints.

"I think he's got an earring."

The jowls appear, the mouth, the neck. An older man, jovial but wattled. The computer has turned his features uniformly gray. Nothing about him jogs any atom of her memory. It's pretty hard to imagine this gray blob pulling off the *fwap-fwap* trick.

"Thank God Mr. Lindquist never took it into his head to get an earring."

They kneel on the floor, peering at the image. And finally, when the face is all there, Prairie Rose turns to her mother and asks: "Well, what do you think, Ma? Is that him?"

HAPPINESS IS A CHEMICAL
IN THE BRAIN

Is it not possible for good manners to exist alongside physical pleasure? Whenever I think of my husband's mistress, the person who pops into my head is the former president of France. He had his mistress and he also had his life as a statesman. His country and his many women. Not mind over body, but mind and body dropped into separate pans of the scale. And the pans both resting on the air. The air that will let neither drop.

Not that I have much faith in the air's good intentions. I happen to have a disease of the sort that will not kill me, a fact that strikes me as unfortunate because, more than death, I am afraid of the whining sap who might emerge from the medley of my pains. In my view, the air is full of chemicals, and as for the mind—well, the mind is a dog that the body walks on its short leash.

That's how I came to sniffing like a hound for any possible mistress who crossed my path. I sniffed Daphne my neurologist and I sniffed Julie, the carpenter who built the

ramp that would get me into the house once I could no longer walk at all. But Julie announced straight off she was a
lesbian, and she even showed me a picture of her lover, and
their child who was born with spina bifida and who wears
braces on her legs.

"We told Lucy the braces would give her superpowers,
like Wonder Woman's magic belt," Julie told me as she
hammered. "We showed her pictures of knights in their
armor and told her how much it weighed."

Of course, I knew why Julie was telling me these stories:
they were meant to be consoling, reminders of the other
citizens who resided in the country where I had begun my
travels. Had she asked I would have told her about the president of France, how he did not hobnob with the masses.
Those who eat *pâté de foie gras* know they are not common.
Part of the pleasure comes from knowing that destiny does
not permit everyone this type of food.

For his last meal he did have foie gras, and also ortolans,
the little singing birds that are an endangered species. He
made a tent by draping his napkin over his head, so he could
more fully inhale their scent. While the rest of his guests
chattered, the president of France sat with his head covered
like a ghost, decimating further the ortolan population by
cracking their bones with the few good teeth that he had left.

∽

HERE IS AN unusual fact about my husband Daniel: he
happens to own a gun—a shotgun from his childhood.

Though for years I protested its presence in the house, recently I told Daniel I'd changed my mind about the gun: it was reassuring to know I had the option of shooting myself when I couldn't bear another day.

But I made the mistake of offering this pronouncement over dinner, as Daniel dished up his lentil soup. The soup, I might add, has a more delicate flavor than its name would suggest. I have asked what the secret ingredient is, but Daniel refuses to say. Coriander is what I suspect.

He began to blink profusely as the ladle dripped: "Perhaps we don't have to discuss this over dinner—"

"This lovely dinner," I added. "Forgive me. You have gone through the trouble of making your special soup, and here I am talking about shooting myself. I forget how dramatic it must sound."

And we never came back to the gun, but in a way we did, because all of a sudden Daniel expressed interest in buying one of the old hunting cabins on the river east of town. "We could use it in summer," he said, "so you don't wither in the heat." He said it came with its own hunting blind, though the plank walkway to the blind was in disrepair. I told him that after thirty-two years of marriage he should know me well enough to know a hunting blind was about as enticing as an outhouse.

"The cabin has indoor plumbing, dear."

"We already have indoor plumbing."

"But we don't have cattails."

"Remind me, what is a cattail?"

Then he showed me a picture. A little dilapidated shack.

It was cheap because it was built in the floodplain, set up on concrete footings. To access it, you ascended a half flight of stairs that brought you to a rickety deck.

When I pointed this out to Daniel he said, "Julie can build another ramp."

I asked why, suddenly, he wanted a cabin.

"I thought I might try my hand at hunting."

I told Daniel I could no more see him hunting than I could see him behind the wheel of an ice-cream truck.

"Why not? I have always been attracted by the idea of sitting outdoors at dawn with a hot cup of coffee and the smell of wet wool filling up my sinuses."

When I tried to picture Daniel's sinuses I saw stalactites dripping.

"What would you shoot?"

"Ducks, I suppose. Surely you would share with me my roasted duck."

"Could I wear a napkin on my head? Like the president of France, when he ate his last meal?"

I was trying to be funny, but my questions just made Daniel twitch. "Last meal? You're not still thinking of shooting yourself?"

"Oh, Daniel," I said as I touched his cheek. "I think about it all the time, but your duck has nothing to do with that."

∾

AND I LET the subject of the cabin drop as he also let it drop: still, in short order, the gun vanished and a strange key appeared with all the others on their hooks. The fob was a yellow rubber fish that could function as a penlight when it was squeezed. I was not upset that he had gone ahead and bought the shack, though I could hardly believe that he wanted a place to shoot poor birds. Easier for me to believe that he was preparing a trysting place. He would never bring his mistress to our house, though in fact I thought this might be all right: it's a big house and we could all play cribbage after.

Instead Daniel spent his weekends at the cabin while I worked here, compiling indexes for nonfiction books. This is how I became acquainted with the president of France— I had indexed one of his biographies. Under *ortolan* there were six entries. Under *mistress*, twenty-seven.

Or I assume Daniel went to his cabin, because he came home smelling of paint. I began to drop names: "I ran into Daphne on her bicycle." But all he said was: "Who is Daphne?" Or: "I ran into Julie in Home Depot," but his response told me nothing: "I saw her Lucy on the monkey bars when I drove past the park."

And so the summer gave way to fall, and the fall I spent on a biography of Aldo Leopold, the grandfather of modern-day ecology. Here's what I know: sampling methods, *Sand County Almanac*, sandhill cranes. I can remember the slots but not what fills them. And the slot for Daniel's mistress remained empty.

I knew if I asked Daniel to take me to see the cabin he would feel obligated to put on a barbecue or take me fishing, though my interest in the cabin had nothing to do with barbecues or fishing. So one day while Daniel was at work I rode there in the HandyVan, my customary means of getting to the doctor and the store. I could tell that Lou the driver thought it strange as I directed him not to any of our usual destinations but toward the dirt roads that ran near the river. When we got to the cabin—which sat with a dozen others in a row—Lou wrestled the wheelchair backward up the deck's wet steps.

"What are you going to do out here?" he asked.

"I don't know, Lou. I suspect I'll just be taking nature in."

"But it's raining."

"Yes, Lou. I've noticed."

He still seemed reluctant to leave, so I waved him off: "The other cripples await you, Lou, they need you to take them to the mall. Come back at four. I'll be all right." Reluctantly he got back in and backed down the dirt road. I sat there waving him off until the HandyVan disappeared.

The river ran behind the cabins, a few of which had been fixed up by other people who must have had real houses for themselves in town. A few more had slipped over the brink of feasible repair. And then there were the desperation rentals, people eking out the winter underneath their mossy roofs, waiting for the flood, the muddy yards studded with broken plastic toys that would be swept away. These cabins showed no signs of life but for the drone of radios buzzing like bees trapped in their windows. The golden oldies. Music for somebody with no place to go except the past.

I stuck the key in the lock and panicked a moment when the knob would not turn—a healthier wife could have kicked the flimsy door to splinters. Stopping to assess the outside of the cabin then, I realized that Daniel had not given much thought to its adornment. No wind chimes had been strung outside, not even a deck chair on the deck. It was as if the cabin had no patience for these distractions, as if it were single-minded in its intent.

Finally, after I backed out the key a smidgen and pressed my thumb to it, the tumblers settled and the door flopped back. Straightaway the scent of mildew slapped its glove across my face. Inside, I found the living room sparsely filled with furniture that must have come with the cabin: a card table with two rickety chairs and a dusty plaid sofa. The shotgun lay on a shelf above the sofa, too high for me to reach.

In the room's kitchen portion I opened a cupboard and found a variety of tins: asparagus, baked beans, cocktail franks. It was not the kind of food I pictured people eating after making love. When I tried, I saw a man and a woman sitting up in bed, spearing beans out of the can, its ragged lid like a miniature sawmill blade sticking up.

Onward, I said, but for a long time did not move.

Out the window, I could see the rain falling. And what tells you it is rain? It's only an aberration of the light. You try to get a fix on a single drop, but as soon as you think you've captured something, it dissolves into the collective glisten. This is a game you can spend a good while playing.

The bedroom door was a vinyl accordion, calamine-colored, screaking reluctantly along its track. Once through, I saw that Daniel had painted the paneling white, the cracks filled so that at first glance the walls appeared to be smooth. Such a funny desire, I realized then, to want smooth walls. That the smoothness makes a difference.

And still, if you studied them for any time at all you could tell that they were only paneling in disguise, the plaster lumpy in the cracks. I wondered if this depressed Daniel, the small ways that his cabin could not help being tinged by sadness, no matter how many gallons of paint he encrusted it in. But then I thought: if you dwelled on sadness you'd never get even one foot out the door. What was sadness, after all, but the fibrous stuff out of which a life was woven? And what was happiness but a chemical in the brain?

Strange what makes you giddy, how similar the feelings of giddiness and fear. When I launched myself, the chair skittered backward through the doorframe of this room too small for anything but a bed. For a split second I was airborne, and when I touched down the mattress swallowed me deeper into it than I expected. The quilt was old and moldy and mossy and limp, made from the underpelts of who knows how many birds—a dozen? a hundred? a thousand?—that obliterated whatever musk could have been left behind by a mere two human bodies when I climbed under it and drew it like a napkin over my head.

Light trickled in through the stitches, but still it took some time for my eyes to adjust. When I looked through the quilt, it seemed as though I were seeing a mass of gray birds in the sky, so thick there were no gaps between their wings. And I was sailing under them, so close their feathers brushed my skin, my arms and legs spread-eagled, my body supported by narrowest of strings. Filaments, I guess you'd call them. Looped around my ankles, neck, and wrists.

I can see that it is Daniel who flies in the lead, but I also know the point bird must keep switching before exhaustion sets in. Soon Lou the driver will take his turn, then Daphne the neurologist and Julie the carpenter. And Julie's lover and her Lucy, flying like Wonder Woman as her braces fall to earth. And even the president of France is with us as we migrate through the clouds, trailing his mistresses like a kite's tail of rags. Even Aldo Leopold is here with us as we fly with the tiny ortolans and his long-necked sand hill cranes.

So it wasn't rain on the roof I heard but the sound of my gray flock, each bird rustling against the others, vying to claim a scrap of skyscape for her own. Despite our scrambling we all flew on, wing to wing, lifted by the collective draft and borne along by each other's wake as we massed in such great numbers that our feathers dimmed the sun.

SLASH (1976)

The slash burners burn the slash to prepare the mountains for replanting. All week they pile the mess of sticks and stumps that last year's logging crews left scattered in the clearings. They build long snaking piles that stand taller than the heads of the tallest men, though here the hillsides are so steep that when they stand on the uphill edge of the pile the top is at their feet. Then they clear a swath of bare ground beside it with their Pulaskis, a tool that has an ax head married to a mattock. At the end of each week someone has to run alongside the pile to torch it with the drip can, which holds a mix of gas and diesel. There's a wick in the spout that lights the drip as each one falls. Then the slash burner runs along the whole pile's length while flames are born around his feet. His feet, her feet, as the case may now be.

∾

THE SLASH BURNERS have always been uniformly young men, though the time has come for them to add some women to their ranks. So this year three have joined the returning five of last year's men, plus two new men who've come from back East. Women, men, it sounds strange to call them this, but what is the alternative? Most everyone is a college student, except for one ski bum and one surfer. It adds up to a crew of ten. The government likes a good round number.

∾

UNDERSTANDABLY, the women are nervous, wondering if they will measure up. They sleep in a trailer that's been trucked into the clearing where the men's bunkhouse has always stood, next to a power pole that is the endpoint of the wire scalloping across the mountains. What has crossed more than a few minds among them is what will happen this summer if any romance sparks. Will they subject their roommates to the creak and groaning of the bunk beds? Will they make the flimsy walls of the trailer sing? Or will they pitch their tents by the creek and let their noises mix with those of the forest, whose own limbs groan softly all night from beyond the edges of the clearing?

∾

THESE ARE by and large hypothetical questions, because among the women there is only one obvious erotic object. Throughout the day, blond strands detach from her braid, mix with sweat, and tangle with the hoops that she wears threaded through her ears. Another of the new women is short, her hair close-cropped to show the muscles in her neck. And then there's Marie, who is knock-kneed and slight, the only slash burner to wear glasses. She's also the one who jumps at the first snarl of the chain saw. Her brown hair she wears in a helmet like Joan of Arc's, but unlike Joan she would not choose to go willingly into the flames. Yet she has chosen. Here she is.

∾

SLASH BURN. Field crew. Coastal mountains. Washington. Marie sent off the application for these words alone, never even inquiring how hard the work was, how much it would rain, how little it would pay. She had a vision of herself as someone in a depression-era photograph, instead of just another skinny cartoon kid from the suburbs. On the application they had posed many questions: could she lift fifty pounds, could she perform CPR. Of course, Marie had lied and answered all their questions yes.

∾

THOUGH THE SLASH BURNERS are newly arrived in camp, already the dampness has caused a strange fungus to grow between their toes. So far they've made and torched just one slash pile, the surfer, their crew boss, taking his turn first. He ran alongside the pile while the flames licked at his tall boots, into which he had tucked his green pants that were made from some unnatural substance that does not burn. Off the side of his one foot the hillside rose and disappeared into the still-standing trees. His other foot surfed on the edge of the slash, which was neither solid nor air but a mesh made of both. For him, the trick to running along a slash pile lay in staying fluid, never coming to rest anywhere with your full weight, not letting your knees lock while the drip can rains its baby flames.

∾

THE SLASH BURNERS all wear the same thing: hard hats, safety goggles, yellow Nomex shirts. But their bodies make these same things look different, the women's hard hats perched awkwardly atop their heads. By the end of the day their faces are black. But their lips, like the rims of their eyes, are stark red, as if their first lips have burned away and these new ones have been made from the insides of their mouths. Their old scorched lips rolled outward, these new lips fixed in place with a hem stitch.

∾

SO A FEW WEEKS go by and they burn a few piles. All the guys from last year go first. Of course, everyone's waiting to see one of the women take her turn, and the women fear that waiting until last will prove that they're afraid. So the week after the last of last year's guys go, the short woman volunteers, not checking the look on anyone's face. She is not fluid like the surfer when she charges straight ahead, a strategy in whose grips she should be doomed. But what saves her is speed: as soon as a leg touches down she lifts it again. She moves like a piston, her calves snapping down and retracting. When she gets to the end of the pile, the others move in to help her step down; then they realize that she doesn't want their help. But they've lifted their arms toward her already, so they change the gesture into the upswing of a comradely slap, but suddenly they're not sure how hard to hit her. They end up awkwardly tapping the back of her shirt. Good work. Tap. Nice job. Tap tap. They can feel the buckle on her bra, which leaves a small singe on the palms of their hands. A spot they need to cool by wagging in the air.

∾

AT NIGHT, in the trailer, the other women come to Marie with their stories. Perhaps because she is the quiet one. Turns out the short-haired woman once halfheartedly tried to slash her wrists, and the erotic object, the tall one with field-hockey thighs, had an abortion just before flying here from the famous Catholic college, Our Lady of the Midwest. Ever since, blood has leaked from her in intermittent drips. She does not think it is enough blood to worry about, but it scares her nonetheless.

∾

THE NEXT WEEK one of the new guys has to volunteer to torch. He has to, because the smallest woman has gone, and so, by laws that are somehow understood by everyone, one of the new guys has to go. The volunteer is a big guy whose body Marie takes one look at and knows is wrong for torching slash. It is too solid, too firmly anchored to the world. Worse, he takes as his example the short woman's unhuman performance and charges down the pile. But he's too big to get away with this, and before he's gone halfway his left leg punches through some brush that overflows the slash pile's edge. Then his foot twists and hooks beneath a branch so that his leg cannot be pulled straight up. Like a finger in a Chinese trap, the harder he pulls, the more fixed is his boot. The others paw his leg for useless moments until the crew boss elbows his way through. He's the one who knows to push down on the foot to make it pop from under the branch that pins it. And from his example the others glean the most important lesson. Which is that sometimes the way out is farther in.

∽

MARIE'S BODY'S STORY is simpler than a slashed wrist, and yet it involves the same idea of transformation. Meaning: as soon as she found out she had the job she started running in a silver suit. The suit was made out of plastic, and the catalogue she bought it from had sold it with the promise that as the sweat flowed from her she'd be able to see the muscles rising below the surface of her skin. On her feet she wore a pair of blue tennis shoes with soles as thin as carpet slippers. She could not run more than a dozen steps before one of her ankles would roll into the dusty pebbles lining the road. Back in her dorm room, removing the suit, she looked at her thigh and pressed her thumb into its creases. At least it looked like there were creases, but maybe this was an illusion, maybe her muscles were just caused by the sunlight's passage through the trees.

∾

ON THEIR BELTS they wore pouches containing the fire shelters they were to use should the fire ever escape from the pile and they find themselves beset by flames. In this scenario the slash burners were to grub out patches of bare ground big enough to fit their bodies before hunkering down, using the shelter like a tent, pinning it with their arms and legs while the fire rolled over their backs. Never mind that it did not seem possible there would be enough time for digging: during training week, they practiced baring the ground and throwing themselves into it. The shelters themselves were no more than foil tarps. Glorified tinfoil. *Shake-and-bake bags*, the guys from last year said. During the training they'd also watched a film about a crew from the Navajo reservation, a group of men who'd been pinned in their bags for thirty-six hours straight. Finally, another crew had come along and told them to get up. The fire had been out for hours. But the men did not believe this until they stuck their arms out from under their shelters and touched the blackened ground.

∞

THE SLASH BURNERS take turns using the chain saw to cut the larger branches. Marie can't help thinking the chain is always going to fly off the bar and catch her in the mouth. Luckily, the other new guy is eager to prove himself with the saw, and only a few other men—and the short muscular woman—will haggle. But one day when this new guy is bucking up a gnarled fir stump he catches the tip of the saw on a knot. And the bar flips up, spins, nicks him in the meat of his chest. Then everyone's swearing about either sex or God as blood spits out and dirty bandannas are pressed to the wound. The boss throws him in the truck and speeds toward town, and for the rest of the day the other slash burners trudge through their chores like pallbearers. Around nightfall the truck gets back and they all crowd around as it pulls in. No new guy: he has to stay in town for minor surgery. *But he's okay*, the crew boss says, and a collective sigh inflates the clearing.

∞

THAT FRIDAY, after the slash pile is built, they stand for a good while watching it, almost as if they expect it to start moving like a worm or snake or other legless creature. The women have made a tactical error: with the new guy out for this week at least, it's only the two of them who have not taken their turns lighting the slash. So they are last after all, and silently they curse themselves for being weak, for being wimps. One of the men volunteers in their stead, but both women insist, rather shrilly, *No*. Marie can tell the blond woman is dying to go: she wants to prove that she is more than just her beauty. She does not wear earrings anymore, because she's been told they might scorch her neck. From the way she holds one arm curled in front of her, Marie can tell that, though she's eager, whatever is damaged inside her holds her back. So Marie says, aloud, *Oh, God help me, I'll go*, which is supposed to be more joke than plea for any serious kind of rescue, though she *would* in fact like to be rescued. Abruptly the rest of the crew claps and hoots, except for the blond woman, who shuts her eyelids in relief.

∾

NOW IT IS HAPPENING too quickly, though Marie can think of no way to slow it down: when she steps to the pile, the boss hands her the drip can as if he were a squire armoring his knight. All she can think of are the Navajos who'd lived at the center of the flame's blue core, saying, *We are alive, so we'll just stay here for a while.* As they told the story in the film of how the fire roared across their backs, the men broke into shivers. Or gagged on their words, sobbing in silence. Never before had Marie seen such big men in tears.

∾

MARIE CHECKS the bottom of her boots, killing time. She sets down the drip can so she can tie her bandanna over her mouth like an old-time thief. When she closes her eyes, she sees herself lying on her back as the fire passes over, her eyelids burning like a piece of film stuck in a projector. Her glasses exploding like windows in an abandoned burning shed. Then she opens her eyes, picks up the drip can again, and peers down into its pure dark. And that's all the stalling she can do without embarrassing herself, so at last she touches her Zippo to the wick that sticks from the drip can's spout. Rolls the flint wheel with her thumb. *Snick.* The wick doesn't catch. *Snick snick.* And then it does.

∾

THRUSTING HER RIGHT ARM awkwardly backward at a diagonal to her body, she lets the drips fall and stands there for one split second while the branches start crackling like gunshots. No going back now, everything back of her is burning. And the pile in front of her looks like a tunnel *whose way out is farther in.* She can hear the flames rising, the green wood moaning, while the slash burners stare at her with doubt and hope scribbled in the twisting shapes of their red lips—

∾

AND AT LAST Marie is left with no choice but to run.

LATE IN THE REALM

On Wednesday afternoons, the Daughters of the British Empire hold their High Tea at Doctor Doodle's Donut Den, whose regular business hours run from five a.m. till noon. They throw some chintz over the tables and stick a silk flower in a jelly jar on top of each, a transformation that somehow lets them feel okay about charging big bucks for sandwiches the size of bottle caps. The proceeds they send back to England, where my mother is originally from, back to some charity for war orphans. I don't know why it took so long to dawn on me which war we were talking about.

"Just because they're elderly doesn't mean they don't still need our help," my mother huffs. She's got the long skirts, the dust cap, she's even got the rolling pin. So it's pretty much a knee-jerk reflex when I put up my hands to fend her off: "Hey, just so they didn't still have their hearts set on adoption is all," I say.

These Wednesdays always throw a segment of Doctor Doodle's regular clientele for a loop, namely the rough trade who have a hard time keeping their a.m. and their p.m. straight. They come stumbling in from their caves hollowed out in the blackberry brambles by the bay; they come because Doctor Doodle's is the only place in town that still offers bottomless cups of coffee. "I can't turn my back on the people," says Doctor Doodle, and I say, "That's why you'll never be a rich man, Doctor D"—this was before I knew about the high-quality weed that he had growing somewhere in the state forest.

But don't go blabbing about this, because the news would break the Daughters of the British Empire's hearts. Or the Doobies, as I like to call them, though my mother has asked me to desist. Doctor D they call "a good boy" whenever they're called on to speak charitably of him, and they have to speak charitably since he's letting them use his shop for free.

Because she lives with Mum, my sister Louisa gets drafted for High Tea duty, though Louisa doesn't go in for any of that *Upstairs, Downstairs* dress-up crap. For Louisa, High Tea is strictly an occasion for navy blue skimmers and her Home Shopping Network earrings, a pair of which she's got to match each one of her good dresses. I think she figures that being retarded is enough of a strain: she doesn't want to have to add worrying about looking weird on top.

The Doobies like to station her at the door, because my sister is surprisingly a Nazi when it comes to body odor and sobriety. That's what happens when you spend twenty years in special ed: you come out an enforcer for the social contract. My sister is the only person I've ever met who knows the correct usage of a cocktail fork.

When the bramble-sleepers first presented themselves, the Doobies took a hard line against letting High Tea be overrun by homeless men, though Doctor Doodle countered by saying that he wouldn't have loaned them his shop if he'd known about their "petty-boojwazh Anglo frou-frou mercantilistic trip." So they've reached an admission policy by group consensus: before four o'clock, Louisa will tell everyone that there's no coffee, only tea, and furthermore they will have to cough up three dollars for the entire pot.

But after four o'clock, when whatever's left is only headed for the trash, they throw the door open, come-one come-all. Stinky Tea, that's what I call this last hour of Wednesday afternoon, which is when I'll also drop in to cop some free leftover scones. A half dozen widows will still be sitting there, eating cucumber sandwiches and draining the last of the Earl Grey from their lukewarm pots, and— though it's probably just a fluke—some of them will even have their pinkies sticking out.

"Four o'clock," Louisa'll announce from her post by the door when the big hand on her watch comes round. And to the outside world she'll holler, "Okay, you guys can come on in for Stinky Tea!"

∾

DOCTOR DOODLE was born Leonard Katzenberg, but that's a hubcap that dropped off a long ways back. Dimly I remember him as a tall kid in the marching band, playing John Philip Souza on his clarinet. But now the Doobies are the only people left in town who still call Doctor Doodle "Leonard," as in: "Leonard's a good boy"—this my mother speaking—"but the way he looks frightens people off." When I observe that the donut business seems to be humming along at a brisk enough clip, she says, "Well, people would buy donuts from Charles Manson if he had any crullers left at ten a.m."

At such junctures, I resist leaping to Doctor D's defense. I'm not exactly eager to have my mother find out that for the past two months I have been doing the deed with Doctor D. We need not go into the pinball game I was playing with him at King Arthur's Reef, where in the frenzy of my being up three hundred thousand points I spilled a Black Russian on the machine and lapped it all up before any of it ran off the edge, the whole time keeping my ball in play.

"Nice tongue," he said.

Black and antigravitational, the Doctor's hair can usually be found stuffed into the crochet job that he prefers to a hairnet, a tam that rides his head like some giant rainbow-colored mushroom. He is the kind of stunningly agile fat guy who moves as if his body were fashioned out of space-age gel, plus he has these very tiny feet I found myself nose to toe with later that night when he helped me climb aboard his boat.

It is, in fact, a boat I sold him, a Chris-Craft cruiser from the thirties, which Doctor Doodle has named *The Elsie*. Before he bought it, the guys in the shop stripped and varnished the deck so the mahogany's highlights gleamed; the hull below the waterline they painted a bright shade of red. Then to push the envelope they dropped in a Chevy inboard big enough to have powered a Cadillac, which when taken up to speed made the boat shimmy like it might splinter into matchsticks. And when it didn't, the guys began to bark and crow in their native tongue, which employs various animal noises coupled with a lot of homoerotic body contact.

This is one of the perks of working in the boat shop: on sunny days, which don't come often in these parts, we'll take turns test-driving whatever's on the lot. Another perk is maybe the thrill of seeing guys like Doctor Doodle—who in high school sometimes had to suffer the humiliation of having a yarmulke bobby-pinned to his frizzy scalp—now seeing these boys peel five thousand dollars from their wads of crumpled twenties. We don't call it money laundering—we just call it selling boats. Because we are rooting for them, you understand, these guys who trade at the fringes of the outlaw realms, who stuff themselves into the cabins of boats too small for anyone with all his marbles to consider living on. And we forgive their haphazard personal hygiene because we know they have to shower in the pay stall at the marina's public john, where they never have enough quarters, these guys who own nothing that takes up space, who wear one pair of sweatpants until the ass wears out and even then they'll get by for months with safety pins dangling back there like a bunch of grapes.

Louisa was with me that night at King Artie's Reef,

so it was the two of us walking beside him as he pushed his old Schwinn down the dirt road that runs atop the levee. You get a cheaper moorage here behind the sewage treatment plant, the sewage a moot concern because the mudflats bordering this whole town stink at all but the highest tides.

"Take us for a ride," my sister commanded. So the Doctor untied the mooring ropes and in no time had us lumbering along at the boat's top speed, into Puget Sound's open water, *The Elsie* chattering so hard I could feel my molars working loose. The lights from the houses blurred into streaks that jerked as the hull went *fwop fwop fwop*. The cabin swayed and the windows threatened to fly off—the transom groaning, the plywood popping—until Doctor Doodle eased up behind the island that is Indian land. He let us drift there while he disappeared into the cabin and eventually rematerialized with a Mason jar full of dark fluid. Homemade blackberry brandy, he said, warning us to strain the seeds by sipping through our teeth.

With the wind died down, I could smell that he must have taken at least one bong-hit in the cabin, the water so still that when we spit the seeds overboard I heard the tiny sizzle of them dropping: *pli-pli-plip*. The jar went round, the shoreline began to tilt, and Doctor Doodle started calling my sister *Ramon Fernandez*.

"That's not my name."

"It's your new name—I just gave it to you." Then he recited from memory: "*Ramon Fernandez, tell me, if you know, why, when the singing ended and we turned toward the town* blah blah blah, I can't remember *the lights of the fishing boats at anchor mastered the night and portioned out the sea.*"

This is what Doctor Do sounds like when he's stoned and flapping off. He went to the hippie state college that was built in the seventies in the woods outside of town: no grades, and everyone gets to make up his or her own course of study. With Doctor D, it was a combination of poetry and plant genetics. After all these years, he often gets the two of them mixed up.

"You're talking like a crazy man," Louisa said.

"No, I'm talking like a businessman. Wallace Stevens, to be exact."

Unlike most of us, Louisa has learned how to cover her confusions. "You don't look like a businessman" was all she said.

The doctor spit some seeds out with a *ffft*.

"That's just your rage for order, pale Ramon. Now everybody shut up for a minute and listen to the sea."

∾

YOU CAN IMAGINE how disconcerting it is when he's there in the kitchen with me and the Doobies, though usually he keeps out of their way by burying himself in his machines, whistling "Rule, Britannia!" as he inserts a wrench into the donut maker's guts. But sometimes behind my mother's back he'll start making googly eyes at me, stroking his beard and rubbing the gold ring that he wears in one ear like Mr. Clean.

And what with these distractions, you can understand why I do not notice right away the man who's sitting with my sister in a booth. It's after four, and I can't tell if he's a hard-core bramble inhabitant—he could have just lucked out in the haberdashery department at the Goodwill store. He's wearing a brown sport coat and a brown hat with a green plaid band. It's hard to reconcile the hat with the man, whose pink face is a little too squirelly for a word like *dapper*. And his head looks sort of deflated and slack, as if a little air has been let out of him.

When I first spot him, I'm in back in the kitchen, helping my mother with an emergency batch of chocolate fudge. At last she glances up, then out where I'm looking through the pass-through slot.

"Don't even think it," she warns.

"Think what?"

"That the two of them look in any way cute."

My sister is following her usual inclination to put four sugar packets in her tea, and when the man dips his spoon into her cup to taste he makes a face that makes Louisa laugh.

Mum wipes her hands on a dish towel before going out to issue some directive that'll take my sister from the booth, in this case a task involving ketchup—I can see my mother demonstrating how to wipe the bottle rims. But as soon as she's back in the kitchen, my mother's plot is foiled: the man gets up and helps Louisa with the ketchup, ha! In five minutes, they're both seated again.

I say, "He looks like Mr. Peepers."

"Those are the ones I'm afraid of."

"I don't think he's worth the worry, Mum. No self-respecting psychopath would wear a hat like that."

Then she gives me a look that's like the knife she sticks in the fudge to see if it's hardened up.

"Those are the ones who think they might be happy with someone like your sister." That said, she tells Louisa it's time to load up, even though by the clock there are still officially twenty minutes left to Stinky Tea.

∽

THAT NIGHT on *The Elsie* and on subsequent nights since, I have climbed the mountain that is Doctor Doodle, his skin shining wherever it's not covered in the corkscrew curls of his black fur. His great bulk fills *The Elsie*'s tiny foredeck, so, positionwise, it usually comes down to this: me on top with nipples stiff from the rank wind off the sewage plant. It's not a pretty picture, but for the inlet we're floating in, and it sure ain't love, I will admit. Something more instinctive and tribal. Something you do because you can.

"While you figure it out, I'll just be grateful," he says. "*Om mani padme hum.* These days I'll take what I can get."

But things are never as simple as guys like Doctor Doodle make them out to be—like when, after these exertions, mainly his gyrating up and down like a marine mammal trying to walk on dry land, Doctor Doodle extracts himself from me. He climbs into the cabin and comes back with something resembling a plastic tackle box.

"Sleep apnea," he explains.

The mask has a breather bag and flex hose running from the mouthpiece. In it, he is a cross between a robot and a pachyderm. From underneath, his voice is Elmer Fudd's broadcast from space: "If I dowen't do dish I fawl ashweep awl day."

Then he plugs the extension cord into one of the power poles on the dock, and the box begins to make a rhythmic *whush-whoosh* as the air moves in and out. Somehow he's able to balance it on the trembling mesa of his belly. And that's how Doctor Doodle sleeps—spread-eagled on *The Elsie*, his bicep a small ham that fills the hollow of my neck.

∾

WHEN THE MAN with the feather in his brown hat returns, I tell my mother, "Don't worry, it's only Hangman." He's sitting with my sister again, business so slow on this fine day that my mother can't even scold Louisa for shirking. "Wino weather" is what Doctor D calls it, weather into which he himself has taken off, leaving a folded scrap that reads, *Grab some cocoa butter and meet me at the Elsie.* From the way my mother hands it over I can tell she's read the note, but is too busy pacing—and every few seconds craning her head toward the pass-through slot—to worry about what's going on with me and Doctor D.

I tell her a little Hangman's never gotten anyone knocked up.

"That's not funny," she says.

They're drawing the Hangman on a paper place mat

Louisa's retrieved from the kitchen, one of the pretensions of High Tea being that the only paper products that can be on view are the doilies on the plates; everything else must be replaced by the Doobies' flowered chintz. Sometimes it touches me to see the melting pot in action via the microcosm of Stinky Tea, the men from the shelter passing the butter patties to the ladies from the fancy condos down the block, while the Doobies glide in white pinafores across the grimy linoleum.

When she came back for the place mat, Louisa also slapped some marmalade on a scone, moving quickly so as not to give my mother a chance to stop her. Afterward, my mother mused tartly, "Is Frederick paying for that, I wonder?"

From Louisa, Mum learned that he goes by the name Frederick.

"Isn't that odd? Not Fred? Not Rick?" she asks.

"You're being paranoid."

"What about the way he never takes off his hat?"

"Maybe he's cold."

She bristles. "I've had a hundred discussions with Leonard about the heat. The thermostat's set at seventy."

"Maybe he's bald. Maybe he's afraid she couldn't love a hairless man."

"Oh, please."

"What?"

"The day your sister moves in with you we'll start having these conversations. Until then, I want you to get out there and intervene."

But instead of doing my mother's dirty work, I stop for a quality moment with Florence Pratt, one of the pastel-haired ladies who come in every week, her skin as fragile as a baby bird's.

"Ooch," I say, parking myself in her booth by the window. "That sun is murder."

The way the years have loosened her tongue has made it hard for Florence to find a lunch date—she doesn't want to share air-time with anyone. Now she starts telling me about how being inside on a day like this always reminds her of the London Blitz: "We were always inside, blinds drawn, the plaster raining on our heads. You kids have no idea what it's like to be trapped in your own home in a city under siege." But my attention is two booths away where the man in the hat is pantomiming a word. Which is, apparently, *chicken*.

". . . my father insisted that meals go on as always. He was not about to let the Germans interrupt his dinner." Pointing to a scar on her lip, Florence says, "This is where I once stabbed myself with a fork."

The man in the hat flaps his elbows.

"Once there was a strike across the street that blew two of our windows out, and my father just sat there, picking glass from his cup. He waited until the rest of us had gotten up from underneath the table, so we'd be sure to see him swallowing the last drop of his tea."

While she's saying this, I try to ESP Louisa about the chicken, but instead of *C* she goes for *S*. And that does it, she's hanged, and while the man in the hat draws the noose, my sister dies in a fit of laughter.

∽

YOU CAN PICK your word for what he is: a weirdo, a wino, a loser, a tard. No one knows for sure what label to slap on him, since the Doobies say as little as they can get away with saying to the unwashed men who stumble in. Oh, yeah, you can talk about the melting pot in action, just like Doctor Doodle can extol the virtues of the bottomless cup, but let's face it: open your heart to those who sleep in the hobo weeds and all it'll get you nine times out of ten is a story that begins with the guy's brain being controlled from outer space and ends with your being hit up for your spare change.

So when on the third week Louisa's suitor comes back, I can understand why Mum announces she's had enough. She's got her sandwiches arranged on a serving platter with a silver stalk that rises from the middle, and she heads out of the kitchen swinging it like a priest swinging incense, something to purify the space when she orders my sister to start cleaning up.

"No, it's not time yet," my sister says. Her words ring in the nearly empty shop, causing the rest of the Doobies to freeze like a Greek chorus.

"Okay, fine," my mother grumbles. "Make me do all the work." When she starts whisking the cloths off the tables,

Frederick stands up to help. He sweeps the ketchup—and the salt-and-pepper shakers, the little rack that holds the Sweet'N Low—onto the booth's seat, then grabs one side of the tablecloth whose other side my mother's already clutching.

"Thank you, I've got it," she says.

"Let me help you, please."

But she insists, "I'm perfectly capable," and to prove it she gives a yank to the cloth, which separates with a chirruping sound. This puts Frederick off balance—he stumbles backward with half the tablecloth in his hands, as mortified as if he'd been caught holding a pair of women's panties. He's off balance enough that he falls into the booth, his feet sticking out, his hat flopping into the abyss under the table.

And it's the hairline that gives him away when he sits up: a peninsula of red hair growing down the middle of his scalp. I know that I know him, only I don't know from where, until finally the voice of Florence Pratt stabs at the air like the fork that once went through her lip:

"Oh, dear, it's him."

"Him who?" the Doobies scream.

"From the paper," she says, raising a finger of one hand while her other hand sets down her porcelain cup. "I very distinctly remember him. In the photo, that forelock was combed to the left—"

"For god's sake, get to it," my mother snaps.

Here Florence withers. After lowering her pointer finger, she brings her napkin to her lips.

"Good lord," she stage-whispers into the cloth. "He's the pervert who's been sent down here to live."

∾

IMAGINE WHAT it must be like to walk his walk, how the past must ride him like a half-ton jockey who will not be shaken loose. Every town he comes to will run another sidebar in the paper, announcing that another pervert has been set free in our midst. And he'll carry that rider everywhere—to the grocery store, the library. The mailman will see him and think: Pervert. The bus driver: Pervert. The police will give flyers to all the people on his street, and they'll squawk the word like chickens: *pervert pervert pervert*.

The Doobies too came from the back of the room like chickens, as if some corn had been scattered at Frederick's feet. They squawked him toward the exit, though what they said was only, *We think it's time for you to leave.* Even when they're dealing with a deviant, the Doobies adhere to their *Masterpiece Theatre* manners.

So you kind of have to hand it to Florence for at least having the courage to come right out and say it. The rest of us would have left him to fester around the P-word like a piece of fruit with a rotten pit. In hindsight I guess this was why he looked kind of shriveled, and also it explained why he'd want my sister for a friend. Someone who wouldn't know the word, someone who didn't read the paper, someone who'd think he looked like a million bucks.

His picture had appeared in the local section, along with the usual chunk of text. Just one and a half vertical inches, enough for us to get the gist: that little boys have to this point been Frederick's weakness. So am I right in thinking that he only wanted my sister to be his friend?

Well, there are billions of people in the world. Let him get another friend.

His mug shot shows him unshaven, his lower lids drooping, his lower lip puffed. This is the hatless version of him that Louisa thumps the next week when I stop into the shop: one of the Doobies must have rooted it out of her recycling heap so we could all cluck over it.

"He tried to trick me," Louisa says as she thumps him with her finger. I can tell that Mum's been drilling her all week, like a prisoner in one of Mao Tse-tung's reeducation camps.

"So long as you were only playing Hangman, you weren't being tricked." I don't know why I'm defending this guy. Even Louisa's impatient with me for being so thick: "I'm *talking* about the way that he *pretended* that he *liked* me." Love—that's what she's getting at.

At least love lite.

"Well, maybe he did," I say. "Like you, I mean."

"But he was bad!" she says—and then I hear my mother's skirts come swishing up behind me.

"Your sister can tell you all about the joys of having criminals for boyfriends," says Mum. "Then she'll show you a copy of her credit report."

With a sigh that's a braid of fatigue and scorn, my mother hands over another folded scrap. *It's ski-time, not*

*tea-time. There's parts of me just itching for you to rub them
with some baby oil.*

"Make no mistake, I think Leonard's a good boy," she
says. But she thinks I could do better.

This is when I dare my mother to help herself to a good
look: the blue bags under my eyes, my hair falling out from
so many bad dye jobs that I look like someone in the early
stages of chemotherapy. Plus on my arm there's this pretty
rough-looking tattoo that was the handiwork of one of my
hoodlum ex-boyfriends: score one for Mum. True, I could
get it removed, but I figure wearing my sleeves rolled down
the rest of my life is cheaper. Luckily, the snake's head on
my hand is not too ragged, and not so much of an embarrassment now that even the schoolteachers have greetings in
an Asian language written above their ass cheeks, revealed
whenever they bend down.

My mother smoothes her skirts and looks away. "There's
no law saying that you couldn't get yourself fixed up."

Louisa chimes in with, "Who's Leonard?"

∽

WINO WEATHER AGAIN, and we get down to the marina
just as *The Elsie*'s pushing off, and the Doctor floors it the
ten miles until we're behind Skoquamish Island in a dead
patch of water. I've brought two big cans of Australian beer,
one of which the Doctor chugs while I catch him up on
Frederick. The other one I'm splitting with Louisa, who
demands that I say, "Excuse me," when I burp.

For his part, the Doctor is waxing tender toward his fellow man. "Suppose the guy was honestly trying to make a clean break with his past? He might have chosen the Donut Den as his best chance for a little forgiveness and love, but you hens had to get in there and muck up his redemption."

"I'm not a hen," Louisa protests. "And I never loved that boy."

"I'm not talking about that kind of love."

"I didn't love him with any kind. That boy was bad."

Then I ask what the hell the Doctor knows about love, and he tells me I'd be surprised what I could learn from a donut shop: "People rising at dawn, delivering their albas, and then what they want is a jelly ball. And they'll walk away with this strange prickly feeling on their skin, wondering: Why is today so different from every other day?"

The hippie state college: that's where he learned a word like *alba*, the song of lovers parting at dawn. You can also blame the college for changing Leonard Katzenberg into Doctor Doodle, and I'd say the odds are against his ever changing back.

"And you know what?" he continues. "That strange feeling is just the powdered sugar on their faces. The whole day, it's only donuts. They think it's love, and what's the difference? Donuts, love, that's the sweetness they taste on their lips."

So much for love, from the mouth of Doctor Doodle. I know someday he'll get sick of living on a boat, and the next woman who comes along with a house of her own, that'll be the one he loves. She'll be eighty-five and wear glasses with a lazy eye patch, but to him she'll be the most beautiful woman in the world, and all because her mortgage is paid off.

But it's hard to see how anyone could get sick of boats on a day like this. Sleep apnea aside, one thing you can put in the plus column of being a fat guy is that you don't need a wetsuit to swim in the Sound. Doctor D has got his butt stuffed into a pair of pink Hawaiian shorts, and, out of nowhere, he does a cannonball off *The Elsie*'s deck. The splash is enormous. His crocheted hat bobs in the waves like a bouquet of flowers.

"Hey, Pale Ramon, throw me the skis," and he also wants the tow rope and for me to take the driver's seat. Then he's squatting there in the water with his ski tips up, preparing for whatever happens next.

What happens next is poetry: William Carlos Williams, a man born with the same name twice, another verse from his days at the hippie college. I know that this poem's not for me but is his recitation to the whole wide universe: *The pure products of America go crazy!*

No, my poem comes a second later, when I slam the throttle and he rises dripping from the Sound, the fur on his body lathered up with drops. Then Louisa lets out a scream of joy that rises above the engine noise, as the Doctor yells for me to give it everything I've got.

ACKNOWLEDGMENTS

These stories first appeared, in variant forms, in the following publications:

American Voice, Crazyhorse, Indiana Review, New England Review, North American Review, Quarterly West, River City, River Styx, Salt Hill Journal, Sycamore Review, and *Pushcart Prize XXIII: Best of the Small Presses.*

A NOTE ABOUT THE AUTHOR

Lucia Perillo's fifth book of poems, *Inseminating the Elephant,* was a finalist for the Pulitzer Prize and received the Washington State Book Award and the Rebekah Johnson Bobbitt Prize from the Library of Congress. She has also written a book of essays, *I've Heard the Vultures Singing,* published by Trinity University Press. Her stories have appeared in literary magazines and have been reprinted in the *Pushcart Prize: Best of the Small Presses* anthology. A new book of poems, *On the Spectrum of Possible Deaths,* is forthcoming from Copper Canyon Press.